Rogue Planet

Randall was at the electronic feelers and the optical instruments, as busy as the proverbial bee. He checked and rechecked to make certain he had not erred. And then he looked into the concerned faces of Donley and Standish.

"How's the captain?" he asked.

A puzzled frown wrinkled Standish's brow. "He's slipped into a deep sleep. Not quite a natural one, yet I know he's had no drug."

Meanwhile, Randall had been learning something he didn't believe at first so was now rechecking. Directly ahead in their enforced orbital course, there appeared to be an object of planetary size and conformation. They were rushing toward it at the speed imposed upon them by the ray stream. It was difficult to determine as yet how long it was to be until the two bodies met, but meet they must as things were now progressing.

He looked up at last from the electronic feeler screen and said to nobody in particular: It's there all right. And we'll soon have to negotiate a landing.

"What's there?" Donley demanded.

"A planet or large asteroid. On dead center in the ray stream. We can't miss it."

"You mean we'll collide with it?" asked Standish.

THE
DOOMSDAY PLANET

by

Harl Vincent

A Tower Book

THE DOOMSDAY PLANET

A Tower Book
Published by
TOWER PUBLICATIONS, INC.
185 Madison Avenue
New York, New York 10016

Later on, Jack Donley was to remember this night's performance by Doris Bright with a strange feeling of awe. Her haunting songs and the feeling with which she put them across had proved to be prophetic. She seemed to him a personification of his fiancee, Mera, who had been lost in space with the Saturnia.

Donley was on the Meteoric because she was the first ethership since the ill-fated Saturnia to take the outside route from Earth's lunar station to Mars. He had watched several months for just such a scheduled voyage, having had vivid recurrent premonitions that he would thus learn what had happened to his betrothed. He'd never believed her dead.

The beautiful singer was abroad for a quite different reason. She was vacation-honeymooning with her new husband, Fred Underwood. Since there was apparent a growing nervousness among the few passengers, Doris had volunteered to entertain them on this the second night out from Luna.

Jal Tarjen, a big bronzed Martian, sat alongside Underwood who, naturally, was closest to the rostrum where his bride was to perform. Behind them was Miss Barrett, an unobtrusive New England spinster on her first interplanetary voyage. There were two very young girls, beyond doubt sisters, possibly twins. Phil Carter, the talkative New Yorker, who had hinted

5

that he owned a significant portion of the Meteoric's cargo, was trying without success to stay away from Lantag, a good-natured but blundering Lunarian who showed signs of mild intoxication. Davidson and Brand, two young computer programmers on vacation, were with Doctor Randall, whose reputation had been earned in his many years of space technology experience. Randall's presence on the ethership was a thorn in the side of the irascible Captain Stark, who leaned against the berylumin wall at the back of the music room, smoking quietly. He had learned that Randall was aboard by order of the World Space Authority and this bothered him. He was a tough space veteran and he didn't need an official monitor . . . even in the unfamiliarity of the outside route!

Several passengers had been taken with space sickness and were in their cabins, which accounted for the slim audience. The crew, those on watch, were at their stations in force. The Meteoric drove on her course.

Donley closed his eyes as the clear sweet voice mingled with the electronic orchestrium organ filling the cabin with magic melody. He closed his eyes to the beauty of this golden haired girl who made him think so much of Mera.

When the last triumphant crescendo ended with a crash of jubilant chords, there was complete silence. Then the applause broke out from the small company of listeners, perhaps too loud and too long.

Miss Bright seemed to sense the anxiety. Rising from the console and silencing the acclaim she questioned Captain Stark. "Captain, would you kindly tell us what the outside route is and why we are taking it?"

With extremely poor grace, the Captain growled, "Doctor Randall can explain better than I," and stalked from the room.

6

Doris looked stunned for only a second; then her smile returned. "Sorry, Doctor Randall," she murmured. "Do you mind taking over?"

Randall unlimbered his lanky frame and jackknifed to his feet. "Don't mind at all," he drawled. He angled to the dais on which the console was installed and faced the mike. Scratching his bald pate, he began, "Folks, the outside route is merely one that is out and away from the ecliptic, which is the plane of Earth's orbit. The orbital planes of our other planets vary only a few degrees from the ecliptic, so most space travel is within these planes and timed to the positions of the bodies. But occasionally there are space storms or other hazards in the usual lanes and then the outside route is preferred, as is now the case. This is just an outer lane, parallel to the ecliptic at a distance of about ten million miles, a longer way but considered safer than the regular routes. It's as simple as that."

A multiple sigh of relief went up from the little assemblage as Randall bowed and returned to his seat. Then a ripple of applause.

Doris caressed the keys of the console and a noble melody rolled from the organ. Her listeners sat spellbound, none more so than Donley. Again his eyes were closed and again his heart leaped with hope. More than ever he was convinced that he would find Mera —alive.

At length the audience gave out with a standing ovation such as this music room had never witnessed. Doris herself was so moved by the demonstration that she could scarcely utter the words of thanks that trembled on her lips. Silently, thoughtfully, the audience broke up and went their ways until only Randall, Donley, and the two programmers remained.

"You know something," Randall said softly, "there was a power here that can not be explained fully. A glorious voice, sure, but a power that came from inside and seemed almost put there by an outside force of infinite capability. A controlling mind."

"A deity, you mean?" There was a hint of youthful scorn in young Davidson's question.

"Call it what you will." Randall's words were thoughtful, measured. "There must be a super-intelligence; this universe of ours didn't just happen. There is too much ordered uniformity, cyclic natural phenomena. It couldn't have merely happened that way." He sort of glared at his listeners as if daring them to deny his hypothesis.

"Something like a digital computer," said Brand without conviction. "You store certain things in its memory and its various outputs can perform the duties assigned. And there had to be a 'you' to program these activities."

"We-ell, not exactly," said Randall, "but the analogy will serve, in want of a better one. What has impressed me over the years is the correlation of natural phenomena that betokens the existence of a lone controlling force. An all-encompassing mind or intelligence, let us say, or perhaps we may even conceive of our expanding universe as an enormous organism of which our solar system is but an atom and our Milky Way only a molecule."

"Sun spots come and go in regular cycles, don't they?" Donley asked.

"Yes and there are tides in the sun itself, corresponding to the movements of the planets. Even hard winters and extra hot summers on earth occur in more or less uniform cycles. Our regular periods of sleep . . ."

Randall stopped short and the others stared. For

there abruptly came a steady throbbing in the beryl-umin floor that supported them. An alien pulsation, a steady beat of uniform pattern and intensity. Pulses, beats, in pairs—not quite equal in intensity. *Lub-dub, lub-dub, lub-dub* . . .

"Like a human heart beat," gasped Davidson. This was an awesome demonstration—of something.

"Well, certainly there's no pump on board that could set up such a vibration," drawled Randall. "It would have to be a reciprocating type and ours are all centrifugal."

Despite his athletic background, Jack Donley had an insatiable thirst for knowledge. He grasped and retained it with amazing facility, whether scientific, philosophical, political or what have you. "Could the pulse come from outside the ship?" he asked Randall, finger on chin.

"It could." Randall mused as he listened and the rest held their breath. Then, slipping to his knees, he touched his fingertips delicately to the floor to better sense the periodicity. "If it does come from outside it would demonstrate the sort of thing I've been talking about, a new and different stellar or nebular throb. What it means—"

Captain Stark burst into the room, red-faced with alarm and puzzlement. He stopped short, seemed to get hold of himself with an effort and, instead of the anticipated tirade, let out with: "What goes on, Randall? Can you find out?"

Randall chuckled inwardly. "I'll try," he agreed, marveling that none of the passengers had panicked.

Donley trailed Doctor Randall and the captain; he didn't intend to miss anything.

In the navigating cabin, Randall busied himself at once with the glittering array of mechanisms that Donley could make neither head nor tail of. Electronic gadgets, optical instruments, a complicated but compact computer. Captain Stark fidgeted and chewed his mustache as Randall worked. The throb was less noticeable here—*lub-dub, lub-dub, lub-dub*—but persistently present.

Finally Randall had the answers. "Captain," he said, "we've been caught up by a cosmic ray stream fifteen hundred miles wide. Its hold is unbreakable, far in excess of the *Meteoric's* total power to pull out. We'll just have to let it take us where it will."

The Captain stood rigid. "How far are we off course?" he demanded with rising inflection.

"Half a million miles," Randall told him.

"Impossible!" the Captain roared. "We must be able to pull out of this ray stream or whatever it is you call it!" He stomped to the engine room optophone and bellowed, "Maximum acceleration on neutrino drive! No rocket ignition until so ordered."

Randall stopped in his tracks. "I warn you," he said, "Don't waste any rocket fuel. You'll need it for landing —somewhere."

Captain Stark harrumped and repeated his order to the engine room. Donley quickly followed Randall out into the corridor. As the full force of rapidly increasing acceleration took hold, they clung to the handrails in order to make even halting progress toward the main saloon. By now the passengers surely would be congregated there.

The ship lurched in an effort to angle out of the ray stream. "He'll never learn!" Randall grunted. "Or maybe he will—the hard way."

The throb was in the floor, the walls, in the very air they were breathing. *Lub-dub, lub-dub, lub-dub,* endlessly, monotonously. But the ship's internal gravity

10

compensators had taken hold and the process of walking was again normal.

All twenty of the *Meteoric*'s passengers were now in the main saloon as Donley had anticipated. The few who had been confined to their cabins with space sickness were in recoil seats; most of the others gathered in small groups, talking, obviously trying to keep themselves in hand. The large congregation made the vibration a little less noticeable, but certainly they had felt the lurching and the pull of increased acceleration and were starting to become fearful.

Randall nudged him and whispered, "Say something to them." He had seen that Donley liked people, that people liked and trusted him, that he was exceptionally endowed with the quality of leadership.

"Like what?"

"They're on the point of becoming panicky. Keep them in line."

Jack Donley moved to the forward bulkhead rail. He raised his voice and immediately everyone listened, even Lantag, who had been roaming about with a vacuous grin and dreamy eyes. "Folks," said Jack, "Doctor Randall and I've talked with the captain about our situation and to reassure you all I'll go get him to explain it himself. Sit tight now." He ducked out the door and those whose voices had been rising quieted down. Donley's confident air had impressed them.

Donley was almost as good as his word, being back in a few minutes, not with the captain but with the stiffly uniformed steward, who had been primed with swift words and a twenty-credit note.

"There's nothing to cause alarm," the steward averred. "This ship has every safety device known and was WSA inspected before we blasted off. Captain Stark is at the controls or he'd tell you himself. He's now maneuvering us out of the energy stream into which we were drawn and there may be more lurching of the vessel. So it will be safest if you all take to the recoil seats for a time. You'll be advised when all's clear."

A few handclaps speeded his departure and those who had not already done so now made for the deeply cushioned seats and strapped themselves in. Donley was here, there, and everywhere, trying to impart confidence, giving help when needed.

Happily, there was no great confusion or display of fear. But as conversation died down to an occasional whisper, the throb from space became more noticeable. *Lub-dub, lub-dub, lub-dub.*

Inexplicable. Ominous. Yet deceptively lulling.

CHAPTER TWO

Donley had been questioning Randall.

"Yes, it's quite likely the *Saturnia* was caught up in this same ray stream," Randall was saying, "but this doesn't help us any."

"It does me. You may think I'm bats, but I've heard this same throb in my dreams of Mera. Whether asleep or daydreaming."

"No, you're not crazy. The close bond between you and Mera set up a telepathic rapport. You're probably gifted with ESP."

Donley didn't laugh. "So you see I've been expecting something unusual. We won't be able to pull out of it, will we?"

"I'm sure we'll not. But what's that got to do with it?"

"We'll land where the *Saturnia* did, won't we?"

"Probably so."

"That's why I booked passage on this ship."

"You do have ESP." Randall eyed him speculatively. "But do you really think you'll find your Mera—alive?"

"I do. I tell you I've seen her in bizarre surroundings. Scared and lonely." Donley suddenly plunged into memories of Mera, of their love. He *had* to find her, he thought desperately.

The computer shows, we haven't changed the situation at all. We are in full grip of this energy stream, going the way it determines."

Randall picked up the tape that was coiling from the logging typewriter and nodded agreement. "Each burst of acceleration and each try at breaking out of the stream has failed, immediate return to the speed and direction of the ray stream following."

"I don't believe it," the captain stated less confidently. "My control instruments indicated one-g and two-g decreases as well as directional changes." He cut back the rocket motor throttles nevertheless.

"Same as shown on the tape," Randall agreed, "but for seconds only, then back to the original."

"I'm sick," Captain Stark averred, turning from the console. He looked it. His color was ghastly and his hands shook. So did his head. Mr. Standish was at his side in an instant, feeling for his pulse.

"He *is* sick," he finally pronounced.

As he spoke, Stark crumpled and slipped to the floor. Donley arrived on the scene and helped Standish pick up the man and carry him from the cabin—to get him in his own bed.

Randall was at the electronic feelers and the optical instruments, as busy as the proverbial bee. He checked and rechecked to make certain he had not erred. And then he looked up into the concerned faces of Donley and Standish.

"How's the captain?" he asked.

A puzzled frown wrinkeld Standish's brow. "He's slipped into a deep sleep. Not quite a natural one, yet I know he's had no drug."

Meanwhile, Randall had been learning something he didn't believe at first so was now rechecking. Directly ahead in their enforced orbital course, there appeared

14

to be an object of planetary size and conformation. They were rushing toward it at the speed imposed upon them by the ray stream. It was difficult to determine as yet how long it was to be until the two bodies met, but meet they must as things were now progressing.

He looked up at last from the electronic feeler screen and said to nobody in particular: "It's there all right. And we'll soon have to negotiate a landing."

"What's there?" Donley demanded.

"A planet or large asteroid. On dead center in the ray stream. We can't miss it."

"You mean we'll collide with it?" asked Standish.

"Not necessarily. If the captain hasn't run our fuel too low, we can land—I think."

Excitedly, Donley exclaimed. "It's where the *Saturnia* landed, I'm sure of it."

Donley closed his eyes and became aware of the *lub-dub, lub-dub, lub-dub* pulsation that was faintly manifest here in the control center. It lulled him into an indescribable feeling of lassitude and lack of concern. He shook his head to clear it and his eyes popped open.

The steward appeared at the door, visibly agitated. "Mister Standish," he told the mate, "some of the passengers are acting oddly and some seem to be overcome. There's a lot of restlessness among them."

Donley was first out the door and clattering along the passage to the main saloon.

The measured beat from space was more noticable here, the saloon being closer to the hull plates of the vessel. It was in the air, in the floor, in everything you touched. *Lub-dub lub-dub, lub-dub.* And it was having an obvious effect on the passengers. At sight of the

15

steward, who was at Donley's heels, one of the young girls screamed and unstrapped herself. She catapulted across the intervening space and hurled herself on the hapless officer.

"You lied! You lied!" she accused him. "We're not getting out of danger. We're in it worse than ever. You—"

Donley laid his hands upon her as gently as possible. "Now, now," he soothed, "take it easy. Everything will be all right."

As she twisted in his grasp and her lithe body pressed against him, he became acutely aware that it was not the body of a child but of a desirable young woman. She subsided somewhat in his arms as they tightened about her. Her cheeks were no longer blanched but took on a swift rosiness.

"Let me go." But she had stopped squirming and looked up into his stern face with a dawning of trust.

Something in her look, her eyes, made him think of Mera and it was just what he needed to bring him back to himself. Was this damnable cadence driving them all a little kooky? The girl clung to him now in what he hoped was a desire to be protected. He disengaged her soft arms and held her away for a better look. She really was a beautiful little thing.

"What's your name?" he asked her for want of something to say.

"Eula," she said, "and my sister is Byrl. I—I think she's unconscious."

Donley rushed to the sister's recoil seat, the steward following him.

"They're from a prominent Boston family," the steward whispered. "Put aboard in my care."

"Get the mate," snapped Donley, feeling for the pulse of the girl Byrl. Eula clung desperately to his

16

arm. It seemed that the sister had passed out—much the way Captain Stark had.

The steward was back with Mr. Standish in a moment, and the mate, acting as ship's surgeon, took over.

"Let's get her in her own bed," said the mate, who had unstrapped the sleeping girl. "Take her sister along; she might panic."

So Donley had Eula on his arm once more but now she was a different girl, jittery and pale, biting her lips. As they rounded a corner in the passageway, a man stumbled toward them with his head down, arms hanging like a gorilla's. Eula screamed and hugged Donley's arm.

The man was Captain Stark and he was muttering like a madman.

"Sick, sick, sick," was the burden of his barely coherent talk. Then he looked up and, seeing Donley with the now sobbing girl, he shouted:

"Where's Randall? Where's Mr. Standish?"

Eula pulled away as the captain lunged forward and Donley caught him in a bear hug. The man was shaking as if with the ague.

"The cursed drumming goes on," babbled the captain. "It's the rumble of doom—and I—we—"

He suddenly hung limp in Donley's grasp.

17

Randall left the navigating cabin with some rather definite data concerning the object that was in their path. Its mass was approximately the same as that of Venus. It had no atmosphere and was apparently the terminus of the unbelievable cosmic stream that was carrying the *Meteoric* relentlessly to its end. From calculated angles and distance and speed, it appeared that they had another six hours to go. Then they would be forced to make a landing—or would crash. Randall refused to consider the latter possibility.

He was surprised to find the captain's cabin empty. It was comparatively quiet, even the pulsations being barely discernible as a mere *ff-ff*, *ff-ff* instead of the thumping rhythm in other portions of the ship. Randall concluded that the lessening of its influence had somewhat released the captain from its spell of power.

Hearing voices in a nearby cabin, he entered and there found not the captain but Jack Donley and the mate at the bedside of one of the two young girl passengers. The other girl sat in a corner, visibly shaken.

"What's happened here?" asked Randall.

Standish looked up momentarily from the girl, who seemed to be on the point of recovering from a fainting spell. "Sh-h," he warned. "This girl went out like Stark did and I think we've found a way of bringing them back—or even preventing it. See the blocks of

18

foam rubber under the bed legs, and the cotton in the girl's ears? This does it."

"It insulated her from the floor vibration and muffled the sound of the beat," Donley was explaining. "She came around fast."

Randall stared. "Where's Stark?" he inquired.

"Across from here," said Donley. "He's out cold again."

Across the corridor, Captain Stark was in the same state as when first struck down. In a deep stupor.

"How come this hits only certain people?" Donley wondered aloud.

"Beats me," said the mate. "But we'll find out eventually. Must have something to do with makeup of individaul nervous systems."

"Guess you haven't seen some of the kooks in the saloon."

"You mean some of the passengers are emotionally disturbed?"

"Understatement of the century."

"Hm-m." It was obvious that Standish was a real medical man.

"Well," proposed the mate, "let's get the captain going again."

"Wait a minute," drawled Randall, entering the room. "First, where do we get all the foam rubber and cotton? Second, won't it be better to leave Stark as he is for a while?"

The mate stammered. To him this smacked of mutiny.

Randall brought out his identification. "World Space Authority gives me the power to take over if necessary. Meanwhile, you Mr. Standish are the skipper. I so authorize it."

19

Randall gave them the facts as he had determnied them in the navigating cabin. Consulting his watch, he wound up with the information that they now had but five and a half hours to prepare for whatever kind of landing they might be able to make.

"One thing I haven't checked," he admitted, "is the state of our rocket fuel supply. And, as you know, we can't land with neutrino drive; it's strictly for steady acceleration in the reaches of space outside planetary gravities."

"I'll check the fuel at once, Sir," said Standish and was off down the corridor.

"And I," Donley decided, "am getting after one Phil Carter. Whether he owns any of it or not, he knows something about the cargo. We need foam rubber and ear plugs or cotton."

In the main saloon things were hardly different than before. Two or three passengers seemed to sleep in their recoil seats. One was muttering in morbid depression. Two more, who had unstrapped and were roaming about, cheerfully chattered nonsense. Phil Carter and his Amanda were holding hands and talking happily of the future. Jack noted that Miss Barrett had become a real good looker. Yes, she had removed her eyeglasses but that wasn't all—you could see that she had been a real beauty in her day. Or was it the pulse from the ray stream that had him bewitched? Miss Barrett, too, reminded him somehow of Mera; it seemed that all females resembled his sweetheart. Resolutely, he turned his gaze from the rejuvenated spinster to Phil Carter.

"Tell me," he demanded, "is there any foam rubber or other vibration dampening material in your portion of the cargo?"

"Foam rubber, yes, lots of it. Sheets and blocks of all sizes. Plastic sponge, too. But why—"

"Let's get it, man!" Donley enthused. "But wait— come along and we'll find out just what is needed."

It took Carter but a moment to loosen his straps and jump to his feet. He too was a different man than when he had come aboard.

"I'm coming too," said Miss Barrett, unstrapping.

The two followed Donley as he went looking for Mr. Standish and Randall.

They were all in the navigating cabin, all solemn-faced as the mate revealed that the rocket fuel reserve was not ten percent above what is required for a normal landing. If anything went wrong such as might require an extra orbit they were sunk!

"We'll make it," Randall averred. Then, seeing Donley and his two companions, he drawled, "What brings you here?"

"Foam rubber. Plenty of it," Donley exulted. "How much and what kind do we need?"

"Enough recoil seats must be protected, and we should resole everybody, whether they are now ambulatory or not."

"Let's go!" Donley could press for action when necessary.

For a moment the scurrying of their departure drowned out the *lub-dub, lub-dub, lub-dub*. But the mysterious pulse was still there, relentless in its effects and its implications.

"How are we fixed for space suits?" Randall asked the mate when the sounds of hurrying feet had died out in the corridor.

"Okay Sir. We have at least twenty-five spares. Do you think we may have to bail out?"

21

"No, I don't expect we'll need the suits for emergency bailout—but you never can tell. We'll need them for sure on this airless planet, though. Do they have rocket packs?"

"Yes. And there's a portable oxygen generator available," the mate remembered. "So we could, if we had to, remain for a long time on this strange body."

"If there are no other dangers—like living enemies." Doc was remembering a stay on the satellite Juno. "But I don't look for anything like that either."

"Like to see the suit lockers and airlock facilities?" asked Mr. Standish.

"Yes, I'd better. Just to be familiar with the layout."

They went below and it seemed to Randall that the steel threads of the companionway were telling him gently, *"lub-dub, lub-dub. . . ."*

CHAPTER FOUR

Donley and Phil Carter came in accompanied by Brand and Davidson, all four loaded down with tools and materials. Miss Barrett followed with a package that seemed not at all heavy, though of fairly large size. Absorbent cotton, no less. Enough for an army.

"We'll have to clear out this room," Jack announced, dropping a couple of wrenches and a bale of plastic sponge. "Have to do some work on the recoil seats."

There was the ring of authority in his voice and the passengers began moving toward the exit.

"Let's get going," he said to Davidson and Brand, who were ridding themselves of their impedimenta. "We'll take the empty seats first."

Again the ever present cyclic quiver was drowned out, not only by the scurrying feet of the departing ones but by the sound of hammer and wrenches as the alterations to the recoil seats were started.

Donley had been wondering what happened to Amanda Barrett, when she swung around the corner of the passageway with an arm clasped firmly about the waist of sister, Byrl, who tottered a bit on what were unusually high-heeled shoes. They were both laughing delightedly.

For that erstwhile owlishly solemn spinster had

23

gone into the girl's cabin and provided her shoes with three inch soles of foam rubber.

That they worked was obvious. What was likewise obvious was the change in Amanda Barrett. Love works miracles. Or was this a side effect of the cosmic pulse? Donley wondered anew; there certainly were differing effects on different personalities; some cracking up, some sinking into a coma, others—like this.

Hearing a commotion in the passageway just outside, Jal Tarjen, who was working with Davidson and Brand on one of the seats, rose up to find out what it was about. Which was a fortunate move, because immediately an entirely berserk Lunarian, evidently one of the crew, burst in on them wild-eyed. On his heels was the steward, whose grasp just missed him.

"Watch out!" warned the steward. "He's dangerous."

Phil ducked just in time as the moon-man swung a heavy iron bar in an arc that would have brained him. Jack and the Martian, coming at him from opposite sides, had the man down and disarmed in short order and then secured him in another of the recoil seats in the same manner as the first man. He quieted down, whether from the effect of the seat modification or from sheer exhaustion was not apparent.

The unremitting *lub-dub, lub-dub, lub-dub,* in the silence following this outburst, seemed more pronounced than before.

"Attention, all those aboard. Attention, please!" It was the voice of the mate, calling out from the optophone audios. The discs were not alight but the voice was unmistakable. "This is a request that all passengers meet at once in the main saloon and that all crew members pay close heed to the optophone nearest them. Randall is to explain what the immediate future involves for all of us."

The audios went dead and passengers began filing into the main saloon. Soon all had gathered together and there was a buzz of excited speculation as to what it was all about. Jack and Phil had hustled the second unconscious passenger into a recoil seat and stood watching him without bothering with the straps. The imprisoned moon-man was quiet and the steward remained standing nearby.

When the large optophone disc lighted up with the faces of Randall and the mate, the main lighting of the saloon was dimmed and the buzz of conversation lulled to a whisper.

"Thank you all," came the voice of the mate. "Before I turn the discussion over to Randall I must ask that any of you whose hearing has been deadened remove the cotton or ear plugs temporarily. All right Doctor, proceed."

"First off," said Randall, "I shall picture on the disc before you what is showing here in the navigation cabin."

There was a click and the faces of the two men were replaced by a picture of the starry firmament with a bright orb in the center which, save for the difference in markings, might have been earth's moon.

"This body," said the WSA man, "is in our path and we will have to make a landing on it. We do not know where it came from nor for what reason, but we do know it is about the size of our planet Venus and that it does not have an atmosphere. We have enough fuel for a landing, as well as plenty of space suits with rocket packs and oxygen supply, also an oxygen generator with which to replenish their tanks. Our electronic feelers and optical scanners reveal that there are living breathing beings there and it must be presumed that they are underground or in surface enclosures where an artificial atmosphere can be maintained. So we do not have too much to fear; we can surely live on this body until the help arrives that has been requested from World Space Authority. WSA is fully advised as of now and will be informed when we have made our landing. Any questions? Jack Donley, you had better take over there in the passenger quarters."

Donley faced the now colemn-visaged groups of people. He saw that the first of the unconscious passengers they had brought here was straining against his bonds and he motioned to the Martian to release him. The second man was sitting up, returned to full awareness. Even the Lunarian crewman was out of his frenzy and the steward unloosed him at Donley's bidding. Those passengers who had been oddballs a few short minutes ago now seemed to be themselves, ensconced as they were in the newly equipped recoil seats. It occurred briefly to Donley that none of these had ear plugs but the significance of this escaped him.

He moved to the nearest optophone voice pickup station. "To me," he said, "it seems the most important question is when do we get to make the landing?"

Several of the nearby passengers nodded agreement. Randall spoke from the disc above. "In less than three hours, Donley. So we haven't much time."

"Well, Doc, we have enough of the seats insulated and will get at the shoe soles at once. Guess the hearing bit isn't so important."

"Watch for that, Donley. The pulsation has strange effects on some. It may be that certain ones will require ear stoppage."

"How about a space suit drill?"

26

"We all went through that before we could board—remember?"

"Yes. Guess there isn't anything else, then." Donley spread his arms wide before the assemblage. "Anything else?"

"When do we eat?" asked Lantag, seeming perfectly sober.

This brought a general laugh and eased the tension.

"Buffet rations have been set up in the dining saloon," the steward told them gravely. "Help yourselves, everybody."

A few sauntered off in that direction. But mostly they remained where they were; not many seemed to have an appetite. The optophone vision flicked off as Doc said over the audio, "I'll be needed here until we land. But I'd like to have you drop around, Donley."

"Will do. In a few minutes."

Brand, Davidson and the Martian asked to go along and the four left as soon as Jack had convinced himself that everybody else was in satisfactory shape—and comfortable.

The room quieted down as they departed and the alien pulse again became noticeable. *Lub-dub, lub-dub, lub-dub.*

Miss Barrett and Phil Carter busied themselves with the task of vibration-soling the shoes of one after another of their fellow passengers. Eula and Byrl seemed to be enjoying a sort of game, the latter taking the cotton from her ears and her sister replacing it repeatedly.

CHAPTER FIVE

In the navigating cabin, Doctor Randall and the mate
were examining the greatly enlarged images projected
by the optical scanners as the surface of the body they
were nearing was explored. It was not an inviting
prospect, that of landing in such a wasteland; there
were no signs of life visible, either animal or vegetable.
The surface was a hodgepodge of bare flatlands inter-
spersed with rugged territory whose mountains were
not strung together in ranges but were staggered
eminences broken up by great jagged crevices in a
manner that betokened widespread seismic activity in
ages past. The feelers had determined that the body
was traveling less swiftly than the energies of the beam,
due to its mass and other as yet undetermined influ-
ences, and that the approach of the *Meteoric*, which
is to say the relative speed of the two, was leisurely as
compared to usual interplanetary velocities. And yet
they would be in the body's immediate vicinity in just
two hours, forty-nine minutes, six seconds as shown by
the last printout of the computer. A relatively leisurely
approach but fast enough!

"What are our chances of making the landing?" the
mate wondered.

"Good, I think," was Randall's reply. "And I think
we shouldn't be too concerned about the lifeless surface we've been viewing. Remember we see only one
side. This body is similar to our moon in that it doesn't

rotate. But we know from our instruments that there is our sort of life—somewhere there. It may well be on the far side."

"Which we will see during our approach orbits."

"Yes, and make our landing where it seems most desirable."

"On the other side."

"I'll buy that." Donley and his companions had come in during the conversation. "It makes sense to me," he asserted.

Jal Tarjen agreed: "Yes, good plan. Will need live pilot takeover from automatic not too late."

Randall and the mate looked at him in amazement. For the first time, Randall noted the tiny gold triple bar pin that marked him as a class A-1 sky pilot and a qualified ship's officer.

"You're a pilot!" exclaimed Randall.

"Yes. Was first mate on Martian ship *Phobos*."

What had happened to the *Phobos* was no secret. Her owners had made a narcotics carrier of her by taking heavy payola from shippers of the stuff, unknown to the officers and crew. All of which had come out in the sensational trials in Interplanetary Court and the ship was now under WSA impound for a period of three years. Jal Tarjen had not recontracted immediately and was now on his way home for a period of relaxation.

Randall whistled. "You may be just what we'll need here a little later on. Which brings me, Donley, to the reason I asked you to come here—what do you think about releasing Stark?"

"Hm-m. He's still the captain," Donley was forced to admit, "and I'd think you're obliged to give him a chance to redeem himself."

"Just what Mr. Standish and I have been thinking.

29

But we wanted your opinion—you seem to have so much influence with the passengers."

Donley saw the point. "I'd say bring him to right now and give him the balance of the time before landing to show if he's got what it takes. We sure have insurance against a mistake, with you and the mate and—and Jal—standing by."

"And yourself," the mate put in.

"If you want muscles," Donley grimaced.

"And persuasiveness," added Randall. "Don't sell yourself short, Donley."

In the dining saloon, about ten of the passengers were standing in little groups, holding plates they had loaded with viands but not seeming in any too great hurry to eat. The steady beat of the cosmic pulsation was quite noticeable here but did not seem to affect any of them. Their shoes had all been modified so as long as they remained on their feet they were protected. Phil and Miss Barrett were here and watching carefully for any that gave evidence of needing ear stoppage. So far, there had been none. The talk was all of the anticipated landing but no undertones of fear were detectable.

Satisfied finally with what they had done, Phil and Amanda drifted over to the table where desserts had been set out. Pastries, puddings, rich tarts and pies— and a large round, three-storied cake with white icing. Amanda gripped Phil's arm when she saw this.

"A wedding cake," she almost whispered, then blushed like a girl.

"Could be," Phil said, undismayed. "If only—"

At that instant the optophone spoke out and Captain Stark's face appeared in the disc. His old look of ill-humor seemed to have been replaced by an expression of benignity. "I wish to reassure the passengers," he said, "as to the landing we will make shortly. We have three experienced pilots aboard and they are presently going over the necessary computations together. In addition, one of these is the WSA man, Randall, who is an authority on space navigation and knows all of its perils and the means of overcoming them. We have two hours, fifteen minutes remaining."

The disc went blank. "Do you suppose," said Phil, pulling Amanda close, "we could get the skipper to—now—hitch us?"

"You mean it?" Miss Barrett had been a beautiful girl, you could see that, but now she bloomed to the even more striking beauty of the mature woman who finds love for the first time.

"I sure do." Phil was already on his way out to find the captain.

And so it was that the music room of the *Meteoric* was the scene of a hastily arranged wedding. Another woman passenger managed to find some white veiling in her baggage. Phil had a ring on his pinkie that had been his mother's, a perfect heirloom to use for the wedding ring. Doris played the organ. It was all sort of mixed up but impressive nevertheless. Captain Stark seemed to everybody to have become a new man, of almost clerical dignity and consideration. All of the passengers were there, also the steward, the mate, two of the chart room crew, and Doctor Randall, who obligingly gave away the bride.

The little wedding party walked up the center aisle as Doris gave out with the wedding march, Captain Stark waiting on the rostrum with book in hand.

It was over in ten minutes, the simple interplanetary ceremony being a short one to read. The captain kissed the bride and so did the mate, the steward, Randall, and Donley—even Lantag. The women made a great fuss over the happy spinster now turned wife.

"I'm a lucky guy," quoth Phil, hugging her to him after the rest had let her go. "And you won't be sorry, Amanda."

"Of course I'll not."

The music room had emptied miraculously so there was not a soul to witness the swift rapturous merging of the two love-starved beings.

With less than an hour to go, Donley and Jal Tarjen checked on all of the passengers and crew members to be sure all were protected against the effects of the pulsations. In all cases the shoes had been altered and with two of the crew and three passengers it had been found advisable to use cotton wads to reduce their acuteness of hearing. Recoil seats in the main saloon were sufficient for all of the passengers and with six additional in case any of the officers or crewmen happened to be in the area when needed. In the crew's quarters and at their assigned posts, beds and seats had been isolated from floor and walls. In case of emergency illness or other reason, ten of the passenger cabins had been prepared by installing the cushioning blocks under beds and chair legs. These cabins were distinguished by a red X painted on each door and their numbers were listed on all bulletin boards.

Captain Stark was in the navigating cabin but he seemed perfectly content to let things stand as they were, with the mate ready to take over the controls when off of automatic and Doctor Randall to take full responsibility. It didn't seem right to Randall somehow; Stark had never been known to react this way to higher authority. For which reason, Randall kept an eye in the back of his head and an ear to the floor, so to speak.

Donley and the Martian remained with the passengers, who were all gathered in the main saloon, eyes intent on the large optophone disc. Donley had promised them that the landing would be put on the video as soon as they were near enough to the body to make it worth while, an arrangement that had been made by those in the navigating cabin. It was merely a matter of cutting in the images picked up by the main optical scanners and converting them to optophone frequency.

When at length the disc was energized, the orb of the body they approached was within a hair of filling it. And, almost before they had time to take in its rugged features, it overlapped and was larger than the optodisc. Randall's voice boomed briskly from the audio.

"Our approach is to be somewhat different than the usual landing approach. This is because of the energy stream and the manner in which it limits us out here. It slows down materially just before reaching the body and sort of splashes around it, much as would be seen if a hose directed a stream of high velocity water against a globe. Where it splashes out is where we will change direction and go into our first landing orbit. At so close a distance, it may be we can land without even one complete orbit—provided we can decelerate sufficiently."

Donley was at the audio pickup nearest to him asked, "Do you plan to land on the other side?"

"Depending on what we see there, Donley. Certainly it can't be a worse place than this side seems to be."

The tortured landscape now seemed to fling upward to meet them. Huge crevices yawned between towering crags just beneath them and then were gone as a flat and dusty plain appeared, teetering and rising at a rapid rate. Then a series of ragged peaks and a gaping fissure of indeterminable length and depth. The only indication that intelligent life may have once inhabited this barren land was an occasional mound of huge size in the flatlands, mounds or irregular outline that might possibly have been the sites of ruined cities. There were no vestiges of roads or of squared off farmlands. Since there was no atmosphere, no wind was there to whip the dust of the wastelands into clouds or those little whirling flurries one sees in California's inland valleys.

The bride and groom, that is the latest pair, sat hand in hand with considerably more interest in each other than in the scene before them. The first honeymoon couple, Fred and Doris Underwood, it must be admitted, were not too far behind them in this respect.

"Prepare for change of course!" came from the audio. The voice was that of the mate, who had obviously taken the manual controls.

There came the whine and then the roar of lateral and underside rocket motors, a lurch of the ship, and the view in the optodisc swung past so rapidly as to become a blur. Then they had leveled off and the landscape below, seeming very near now, slid swiftly sternward. There showed a sort of bluish haze as if they were in the midst of a light fog. The angle of flight evidently changed ever so slightly, or Randall had altered the angle of the optical scanners, because the horizon became visible up ahead. Here the blue haze seemed to be merging with another that had a distinctly pinkish cast.

At this point Randall came to the audio again and asked for Jal Tarjen. Told him they wanted him in the navigating cabin. "Nothing in the way of an emergency," he added hastily. "But we want you on hand. I've not forgotten you're a top grade pilot and it's a good safeguard—"

"How about me?" Donley asked hopefully.

"You're best right where you are," Randall told him. "Remember our conversation. And thanks for standing by."

"Oh, well, I'm no spaceman," Donley was forced to admit. But he'd have given his right arm to be nearer the scene of operations.

The Martian unstrapped and disappeared into the corridor. The audio let out with Randall's voice once more. "The pink haze you see at the horizon," he announced, "is evidence of another energy that is splashing partly around the body from the opposite side. We hadn't known of this before and what it means we aren't sure as yet. However, we do know two things about it. The second energy is lesser than the one we are in. And the merging of the two in space surrounding the body will assist us in landing."

Again came the rising whine and then the roar of forward rocket motors, the automatic 180 degree reversal of the recoil seats and the switching of the view to the optodisc on the rear bulkhead as deceleration began. There was the usual illusion of still facing forward. Donley thought of the ever-present throb and it came to him that he hadn't noticed it at all since the start of the landing operation. Deliberately he tried to pick it up out of all the other sounds, but he could not. Only by dropping his hand to the floor beside his seat and touching it with his fingertips was he able to apprise that it was still there.

The retro rockets continued their roar and the landscape below was slowing down in its apparent motion.

Ahead toward the horizon could be seen what looked like a large bubble that glowed in the swiftly darkening sky. Then they had crossed the dividing line between day and night and were in Stygian darkness. Only the distant bubble could be seen. Apparently they were heading directly toward this phenomenon.

And then the *Meteoric* rocked to a terrific shock as one of the rocket motors exploded. There were sounds of ripping metal that were quickly drowned out by the cries of the passengers. Then the lights went out and Donley unstrapped himself and rose up in the darkness.

"Take it easy, folks," his calm voice sang out, "I don't believe this will be serious but I'm going to find out the score."

Fred Underwood spoke out of the dark, "I'll go with you."

"Not a chance. You stick with Doris. And everybody sit tight until I let you know what's what." He had already tried the audio and found it dead.

As the passengers quieted down under his urging, there could be discerned faintly the cosmic pulse. *Lub-dub, lub-dub, lub-dub.*

The lights flickered on as he darted into the passageway, glowed redly a moment and then came up to full brilliance. An emergency generator had taken over.

CHAPTER SIX

The Martian was with Randall at the controls and the mate was calling out numbers from the tape as it chittered out from the alarm printer of the computer. Captain Stark was nowhere to be seen, which was a strange if not ominous circumstance.

"Where's Cap?" was Donley first question.

Randall partly turned from the controls. "Wish I knew," he admitted, "two of the crew came and whispered to him, then all three slipped out."

"Could he have caused the explosion?"

"No, but he might have jimmied the power and light circuits."

"They're all right now, aren't they?"

"Yes."

"How about fuel for landing?"

Randall held up his hand as Mr. Standish called out more numbers. "A bare sufficiency remains," he said. "We'll do it, I swear. But I sure wish I knew about the captain and those two—"

Donley was watching the deceleration indicator and trying to see the view in the optodisc at the same time. Up ahead the glowing bubble was growing larger with increasing rapidity, it seemed, even though they were slowing down to near landing speed and dropping surfaceward.

"I'll go looking for them if you want," he offered.

"Thanks, but I wouldn't know where to start."

37

The roar of the braking rockets continued, a little more subdued as Randall inched back the main throttle. And then a new lurch of the ship betokened a new happening. It was as if a considerable weight had been jettisoned very suddenly and Donley saw Randall's face pale with realization.

"The auxiliary rocket ship!" he exclaimed. "They've blasted off in that."

The blue flame of the single rocket exhaust showed then in the optodisc and vaguely outlined ahead of it the small stubby-winged hull of the emergency escape ship. It was dropping faster than they and veering away from their line of approach.

"Why? Why?" the mate was gasping. "I don't—"

"Never mind why, just now," Donley interrupted. "Back there in the saloon there are some people ready to panic. What to do about that?"

"I'll put our landing image on their optos," said Randall. "The escape ship is out of sight now and they needn't know about that. You can calm them, Donley. Just keep their minds off of things by describing the landing as you watch it—back there."

Donley took the hint and scuttled back along the passageway.

He had been right about the danger of panic. The optodiscs had not yet been reenergized after the blackout and a bedlam of shouting greeted him as he entered. Numbers of the passengers had unstrapped and were milling about. Donley was amazed to see that Brand and Davidson had teamed up with Eula and her sister Byrl. More effects of the ray stream pulsations?

"Quiet! Quiet!" he boomed. "I've been at the con-

38

trols and everything's all right. The optodiscs will show—"

At that instant, the large disc aft glowed into life for all to see that they were approaching what now appeared to be a transparent dome of great size, lighted within and obviously an enclosed space for living quarters of some sort. This sight had more quieting effect than had Donley's voice.

"You will be glad to know," he told them, "that Doctor Randall himself is now at the controls. And he's one of the top men of WSA. He swore he'd make this landing safely."

He watched as Brand buckled the safety belt of the recoil seat in which the girl Eula had reclined, then strapped himself in the seat alongside. Davidson was doing the same with Byrl. To Donley this was a surprising thing for the steward had told him these girls were sent on this trip by parents worried because of their withdrawal from contacts with the opposite sex and more than normal preoccupation with each other. And the two young programmers had vowed eternal bachelorhood! What next would the ray stream accomplish?

The view in the optodisc now showed a faintly star-lighted landscape beneath them. It was seemingly not as rugged and menacing as that of the other side of the body and was slanting up toward them and was slipping sternward at what Donley thought was just the proper angle and speed for a perfect landing. If there were to be found a smooth spot ahead. The lighted dome was a mighty inviting sight.

Seeing that the last of those who had been on their feet were now safely buckled into recoil seats, he followed suit. "You will notice," he said quietly from where he sat, "that everything is perfectly normal for a good landing. The braking rockets you can hear are lessening their power at the correct rate; Randall's got it made."

As he spoke, the diminishing roar of the forward and underside rockets ceased entirely. They had run out of fuel! But Donley kept the thought to himself. Randall fired the emergency solid fuel braking tube until it, too, was silent. They had slowed almost to landing speed. Underneath and just ahead was a considerable area that looked smooth and of sufficient size for landing. They were skimming the surface.

"We'll be landing at once," Donley opined. "I'd guess that we may have a slightly bumpier contact than is customary; after all this is no ethership port. But it shouldn't be too bad."

He hoped against hope that he was not faking so much as to be noticeable. Actually he wasn't at all sure himself.

And rightly so. They struck once and bounced high, then again with a grinding sound, slewed to one side and then the other, bumping solidly then with a screech of tearing metal as hull plates let go in a rough slide over the terrain they could no longer see. Donley pressed so deeply into the cushions of his seat that he felt momentarily suffocated. He heard one of the recoil seats rip loose from its pedestal and go slamming against another. A man screamed horribly and the *Meteoric* turned slowly and majestically on its starboard side, stopping with the deck at an angle of at least thirty degrees.

Partially stunned, Donley could only sit there and marvel. He did not unstrap until the cries and babbling of the passengers grew to such proportions as to hammer at his eardrums painfully. Then, slowly as if in a dream, he unbuckled his restraining belts.

Randall was calling out over the audios: "Everybody listen now. We're not in too bad shape. The lower deck plates are holding, so far as air tightness of the upper hull is concerned. But you must all get to the space suit storage and airlock as soon as you can. The mate and I'll be there to help; so will Jal Tarjen. Jack Donley, will you take over again back there? Get them organized?"

"Sure will, Randall." Fully himself again, Donley heaved up mightily, holding to the seat backs to keep his balance on the sloping deck plates.

In a moment Fred Underwood and Phil were with him, offering help. And, of all those aboard he would have least expected, Lantag—sober as a judge. All three goggled as the Lunarian pulled a bottle of Martian chulco from his pocket and sent it crashing against the bulkhead.

The faint pulse told with its *lub-dub, lub-dub* refrain that still another cure had been effected. At least this was the way it seemed to Jack Donley. A mysterious thing, this rhythm.

Randall had originally called it a stellar or nebular throb. Could it possibly come from such vast distances as this implied? And what was its nature? Was there a purpose? Donley had to give it up.

While these thoughts raced through his brain, he was straining from seat to seat up the sloping deck, followed closely by Fred and Phil. Perhaps even Lantag was trailing them. They found the man who had let out the scream when they crashed—he was wedged between two of the recoil seats, his own evidently having been torn loose by the shock and catapulted

41

against the other. He was unconscious, still breathing but with what looked like a serious head injury that bled copiously. His limbs were sprawled in impossible positions and it was obvious to Donley that this betokened broken bones. In addition it looked as if the man had a crushed chest. The others were eager to try and extricate him from the smashed seat members but Donley decided he simply must not be moved. He managed to climb up the slope to one of the optophone audio pickup stations and got word to Randall, describing the victim's apparent condition.

The mate came in on the conversation and promised to take care of the situation and make the injured man his personal responsibility.

By now, most of the passengers had unstrapped and were trying to get away from where they had been, anywhere to be on the move. They slid and scrambled over the tilting deck, bumping heads, shoulders, and knees against the seat pedestals and mouthing their disgust or expressing pain. It was a bedlam of pointless confusion, getting them nowhere.

The magnetic balancing controls of the ship began then to take hold and the ship gradually righted itself to the extent that there was less than possibly three degrees of list. The confusion diminished enough so Donley could make himself heard. Randall and the mate had joined him by now.

"Take it easy, folks," he called out. "Let's get set to go places. There's no air outside so we'll have to get into space suits and through the airlock. Randall and I'll get the move organized."

As usual, his calm voice brought results. There was enthusiastic approval from the listeners. Anything was better than just milling around. And there was intense if fearful curiosity about the strange world on which they found themselves.

"What do we do?" a woman's voice asked.

"First we'll have to check the lists, passengers and crew. So let's all of you stay put till we're ready to go out. Okay?"

There was a chorus of good-natured agreement. Donley saw Mr. Standish at an audio pickup station and almost at once two crewmen entered with a stretcher. With extreme care, the injured man was moved to this. The mate gave him a hypodermic shot.

"Should keep him out until we can fix him up," he told Donley. His voice lowered and he moved close. "I sure hope there's a place in that dome to take care of him," he added.

"Can't do it here—in the ship's hospital?"

"We're losing air,"—a whisper. "Sprung a leak, levelling. Compressors and oxygen going full blast and still we're losing pressure."

Better keep quiet about this, Donley decided. But they'd have to get moving. "How long do we have?" he asked the mate.

"Little over an hour." Randall nodded confirmation of the mate's words.

Standish was already checking off the passengers on his list. "I'll round up the crew now," he said. "Want to come along, Donley?"

"Sure thing." Turning to Randall, he asked him, "Keep your eye on things here?" Donley rubbed his chin, a habit he had when distressed.

Randall nodded and Donley slipped out with the mate. Naturally, Stark and two members of the crew were missing—those who blasted off in the emergency escape ship. Or so they thought. But the steward was likewise among the missing. So they started breaking down locked cabin doors, the big Martian having come along just in time to be of great help. They hit the jackpot in four tries, finding two dead crewmen in one room and the steward himself, alive and burning with rage, in another.

"Knocked me out, the captain did," he raved, "with two phony crew men grinning beside him. Where is he? Where are they?"

They got the story then. The two with Stark were not crewmen at all but were stowaways who had made up to look like the two real crewmen who had been strangled. The steward had awakened in a cabin not his own and remembered that the captain had acted like a maniac when attacking him, more like a zombie —as if drugged or hypnotized.

The injured man, still on the stretcher, had been laid by his two bearers on a table in the dispensary. Three more of the crew were now located and this completed the list.

"That does it," the mate said. "And now I'll have to give this man some first aid so he can stand being crammed into a space suit."

He went to work at once with the two stretcher bearers and the big Martian standing by. Donley returned to the main saloon, with the steward.

"We'll be ready for the getaway in a few minutes," he told the passengers, then apprised Randall of what had transpired.

"So-o!" exclaimed Randall. "A light begins to dawn. You know, Donley, the WSA had a tip before we left that something funny was being pulled on the *Meteoric*, something illegal but of unknown nature.

44

I'm supposed to find out what it is; how do you like that?"

Donley stared. "Of course I'll help," he offered.

Randall laughed softly. "You would," he said. "And maybe you can if and when the time comes."

Things moved fast after that. The mate, followed by his two stretcher bearers and the other three of the crew came in and stopped by Donley and Randall.

"You've gotten him into a space suit," Donley exclaimed.

"Right. And bandaged as well as possible. We're all set now."

Donley moved to the corridor door, Randall alongside. "Follow us in small groups," he instructed the waiting passengers and crew. "Not more than four at a time, but as fast as you can make it. The first group will include the mate and his patient. The man is badly hurt."

Randall whispered, "I'll stay with you till you get things moving at the airlock. It's a little tricky donning the suits and operating the lock, you know. But then I want to be back at the instruments for a few minutes."

Donley assigned the steward and Jal Tarjen to make up the first group with the mate and his patient and they moved off into the corridor.

He then called to Doris, who stood a short way off. "Better follow them, Doris," he said, "in say five minutes. Get Miss Barrett and the two girls to make up your group. Fred and Phil will help me."

He ducked into the corridor with the two men trailing him. Adding up the lists, he found, in addition to the passengers, there were the steward, the mate and five crewmen included, making twenty-eight in all to

45

be taken care of. With luck, they'd save them all—including Randall and himself of course.

Randall was explaining the mechanism and use of the airlock, while the mate demonstrated the complexities of space suits. The injured man had been deposited on the floor by the lock entrance.

"Better crowd two groups through the lock each time," Randall advised Donley. "That way we'll conserve some air."

By the time the mate, the steward, and the Martian had been suited and their faceplates bolted home, their oxygen and communicators turned on, Doris and the other three of her group were there—all four a little pale. Silent, even the two girls. Donley told Fred and Phil to get them suited and then returned to the main saloon to set up the rest in groups. By now, exertion was making him a bit short of breath and if he moved too fast there was a sense of suffocation. Air getting short—and maybe bad.

Back to the airlock after assigning group members, Donley did all he could to speed up the rescue operation. Two groups at a time, as Randall had suggested, went through the lock, accoutered for the vacuum and cold outside. A few had complained they were breathing with difficulty and Donley saw that cyanosis was setting in with Fred and Phil, their lips showing bluish. He sent them through with the next charge of air that was lost when the outer manhole of the lock opened. Only one group remained when Randall arrived from topside and he helped in their sendoff.

"Air getting contaminated," he told Donley, "and pressure down to about four pounds."

"Okay, okay." Donley saw the heaving of Randalls chest and the blue around his lips. "Here, get into this suit quick."

46

By the time they were suited, it was with vaguely groping fingers and with his mind going blank that Donley was able to shut his own faceplate and turn on his oxygen. Another second, he was sure, and he'd have passed out. He breathed deeply and gratefully inside his helmet as they went into the lock, Randall clamping the entrance manhole shut behind them. Donley recovered swiftly now. Good old oxygen!

"Good thing I'm along," Randall's voice grunted in the helmet communicator. "I clean forgot to tell you how to operate this from inside." He pressed a wall switch that was high up out of the way, the outer door swung open and they went through to join the others.

CHAPTER SEVEN

Coming out from the light into the night of the alien planet, Donley could make out nothing of his immediate surroundings at first. There was a subdued rumble of conversation in his helmet communicator, so he knew that many of the survivors—he hoped most of them—were close by. Off in the distance and at a higher elevation was the glowing dome, outlined against a background of velvety sky with a myraid of stars, brighter than on earth and shining without a twinkle. Hardly recognizable because of their steady brilliance and far greater visible number. Then two double streams of rocket flame arched up toward the dome, about half-way there. Another and another alongside, flashing intermittently.

"That," came Randall's voice, "must be the mate's group. He's towing his patient and the other two are right beside him. Good!"

With eyes becoming accustomed to the starlight, Donley could now see the huddled groups of weird figures nearby. Figures similar to men only in that they had two legs and two arms. Bodies bloated to incredible size were of course the vacutex fabric suits expanded in the pressureless environment. The oversized round heads with the thick tentacles protruding above were the helmets and their communicator antennae.

48

"Why has nobody started but the first group?" Donley inquired.

Several voices answered in his communicator. "The mate was in a hurry." "We were waiting for you, Donley."

Donley could now make out each and every figure but, naturally, could not identify individuals. The trails of the first group's peroxide-powered rockets had now reached the dome and he estimated it was about two miles away. And up a rugged slope that would have been a hazard on foot, would take hours to negotiate.

"Come on folks, let's go!" he said into his helmet. "A few at a time and the sooner the better."

A pair of the weird figures clinging together some fifty feet away, rose up on twin flares from their rockets, heading for the dome. Must be Phil and Amanda, thought Donley. Or for the matter it could be Fred and Doris, Brand and Eula, or Davidson and Byrl. He chuckled inwardly as he enumerated the couples, then sobered suddenly as he thought of Mera. She had to be alive, just had to be here in this incredible world. He activated his own rocket pack and soared upward in an arc toward the dome, with another figure beside him.

"That you, Randall?" he asked softly.

"Yes. Thought I'd keep near you."

"Thanks." The starlight now seemed considerably brighter than the light of the full moon on earth and they could see clearly the nature of the surface over which they were passing. It was a shambles of ancient rubble, obviously the ruins of a hillside city which had been destroyed by nuclear means. Fire storm.

"See that, Randall?" Donley asked. "How long since the bombs caused that?"

"Many generations ago, I'd say. And my guess is the dome up there tops the subsurface refuge of the survivors' descendants."

Awed by the enormity of it, Donley realized that a last great war had been the death of the planet. "Hope we're welcome there, Randall."

At this moment, the area around the dome was brilliantly floodlighted and they could see that a spacesuited figure had emerged and was formally greeting the first groups of arrivals. This figure looked not too different from the others, disguised as they all were in the bulky space outfits. The man, for man it must be, moved closely to the one that held another bulk in his arms—the mate with the injured man he had towed along with him. Immediately, the stranger helped with the burden and led the way into an opening that gaped in the side of the dome. An airlock. The opening was closed then, leaving two figures outside. Two other figures were just about to drop, rocket-braked, at the base of the dome—the two who clung together.

Donley and Randall were coming in with short retarding blasts from their rocket packs. "You down there, Tarjen?"

"Yes, and our steward. These others—"

"—are Fred and Doris Underwood," a laughing feminine voice supplied.

Others were arriving not far behind as Donley and Randall dropped beside those already here. One came over to them; it was the Martian.

"Man who take mate inside show us how to work airlock. Come."

This was a large airlock and held all who had so far arrived from the Meteoric; it could have included Jal Tarjen easily but he remained outside to operate the mechanisms. So there were only Randall and the steward, Donley, and Fred and Doris going through this trip. There would be a second load in a very few minutes, then others as the rest arrived from the scene of the wreck. Half of their entire number could well have been accommodated in this lock, had they been ready to enter.

As the inner door opened and air rushed in, Doris was first to get her helmet off and her perky countenance was a joy to behold as she shook out her golden curls.

"Where's our monotonous drumming?" she asked. "I don't hear it."

Donley had his faceplate open and was sniffing the air experimentally. It was fresh and breathable, apparently not much different from what they had been adapted to. "I had wondered about that too, Miss Doris," he said, "but I suspect lots of things will be different here."

The others were passing through the inner door of the lock into a sort of rotunda that was softly but amply lighted. Donley was last to enter a new environment and he sealed the inner door so the lock could be opened from outside. Meanwhile, Doris had stripped off her vacutex suit and kicked off her shoes with the foam rubber soles.

"No lub-dub," she declared, standing with stockinged feet wide.

Fred was not far behind in getting back to normal attire and he soon confirmed her finding. But Donley was not so sure. Watching the steward struggle with the sealing seams of his vacutex, he cocked his head to one side. No, he couldn't hear the pulse and he couldn't feel it in this floor. But somehow it was there, beating at his brain with its infernal rhythm.

Lub-dub, lub-dub, lub-dub. No sound, no mechanical vibration, a hammering at the consciousness only. And it was all around him.

Many doors were set in the wall of the rotunda and all were closed. The newcomers had no means of knowing through which one the stranger had taken Standish and his patient. No other strangers appeared. But another group of seven or eight from the *Meteoric* was coming in through the airlock.

A door swung wide just across from them and the mate came out. He was in surgical white and a mask covered the lower portion of his face. He motioned to Donley and Randall.

"Come in, both of you," he said. "Want to show you something."

It was an operating room they entered, but equipped like no operating room they had ever seen before. Same sort of table and similar lights above it, but no anaesthetizing equipment, and the glass-doored cabinets held instruments of entirely unfamiliar design. The patient was nude, on his back, unconsicous but breathing regularly as if only sleeping. Over him bent a man in white, with a crop of bushy red hair topping his head, and he was just straightening a twisted right arm that was gory with compound fractures. Randall and Donley watched intently as he worked the bones into place, then seemed to just spray the union with a pistol-shaped contrivance that gave out a high-pitched sound but showed no visible emission. The bones just fused together as if by magic, leaving no trace of where the jagged breaks had been. There was no blood, the artery and large blood vessels having been sealed off, not with hemostats but by some method which invisibly closed the ends as if they had been pinched shut and welded. The amazing surgeon worked with great speed, his fingers literally flying as they tied the main artery and several of the large veins, then closed the gaping tear of a wound. He did not speak, even to ask the mate for assistance, but discarding his pistol-like device, he picked up another glittering instrument from the tray, this one somewhat resembling an ordinary stapler. Rapidly pinching together the edges of the wound with the instrument, which was obviously a super-modern suturing device, he finished with a completely closed wound that showed no scar nor any other evidence of where it had been.

"Look at the patient's head," whispered Standish.

Where the ghastly injury had been there was now only a patch of bare skull a few inches in diameter, where the hair had been removed. No scar or other evidence of the original lesion.

"Fracture and concussion," the mate told them. "He —Apdar he calls himself—did a miracle of brain surgery, returning the trepanned bone and closing the wound as you've seen on the arm. Six broken ribs too, but luckily no internal injury. Not a mark on the chest —see?"

But Apdar was already at work on the patient's left leg, where he performed another miracle of surgery. In ten minutes he was finished and the leg was good as new. Then he drew a small hose with a glass nozzle from a whirring little pump of some sort that was beneath the tray. A short puff from the glass tube into each of the patient's nostrils and the man sat up.

"Where am I? What happened?" he demanded, blinking in the bright light from overhead.

The mate was beside him, trying to explain, helping him off the table, then into his clothes. Apdar, stepping out of his white gown and removing the antiseptic mask, proved to be a rugged-appearing human with square jaws and steel-bright eyes set in unusual width beneath a corrugated brow. His expression was gloomy, sad, not at all flushed with success as would be expected.

"You've done something wonderful here," breathed Randall.

"Sure have," Donley agreed. "I couldn't believe it when I saw."

"Apdar likes not to see people suffer," was his only reply.

"English, you speak!" exulted Donley. "Did you learn it from some survivor of an earlier wreck—the *Saturnia?*"

"Yes, my friend."

"Then where are they—the survivors?" Donley could not contain his excitement.

"A long story is required. Apdar is tired but will explain as we go along." The man tottered a bit and raised a hand to his head.

For the first time, Donley noted that he wore a slender chain around his neck and from this depended a medal or locket which he now fondled as if it might be a charm.

Apparently it was just that, because Apdar straightened his back resolutely, color returned to his cheeks and he walked steadily to the door.

"Come, friends," he said then. "Your companions will be assembled with us in amphitheatre and explanations are to be exchanged. Not?"

What he had called an amphitheatre turned out to be more like a nightclub bowl in Los Angeles—or Oklahoma City for that matter. A small stage with lectern and microphone, set down from a semicircle of seats that were comfortably upholstered and numbered probably one hundred and fifty. The visitors filled the first two rows down front and were exceptionally quiet when Apdar stalked down the center aisle to the microphone. There was no other human of his kind with him or even in sight. His first words told them why.

"I am the last conscious being of my kind," he told them. "I do not say last alive, you see. Others not dead but what I call living-dead. And for a reason. My planet, Ormin, is doomed. So is everybody here, even you people. Ormin, once outer planet of system Sirius, was dead body many generations since—by total war between east and west. Then flung from orbit into space and now riding a galactic energy beam to collision with another body which destroys both with completion. It is the end of our world, of us all. In vision I told by—how you say it—informant—a means of putting all peoples here into the state of living-death so they not suffer mentally before, neither physically at time of. It is a throbbing force that surrounds us and some have been struck down sooner than others by this. I am the last."

He drew himself up proudly and continued. "My people descended from powerful eastern territorials of Ormin. Who destroyed the west but had to go down here to escape retaliation, you call it. I say down here means below this dome where many levels hold the living-dead and machines that keep air and provide food if needed. Apdar only one now who needs and he too go soon. Because destruction comes quickly now."

His alarmed audience burst into bedlam as if on a signal. This simply could not be—the man must be daft. They can't do this to us. But Donley was putting two and two together; cocking his head, he could feel

55

the *lub-dub, lub-dub* of the energy pulse. Adpar was giving himself credit for a natural phenomenon. Or was it natural? At least the thing was in space and not humanly controlled. It did seem to act or be manifested differently here than on the *Meteoric*.

The little hall was in pandemonium now. Some of the visitors were objecting. Others agreed that there was the lub-dub effect in their own consciousness, even if not heard or felt. Others just wanted out.

Apdar stood before them, silent, rather abashed. He looked pleadingly to Donley and Randall where they sat. Help me show them the truth, he seemed to be imploring with those sad eyes.

Donley was on his feet, facing the room. "Quiet, people," he requested. And there was almost immediate compliance. "Apdar knows his onions," Donleys continued. Maybe he's right, maybe wrong, but we owe him respect. And our own Doctor Randall will check what he says. Meanwhile, we're all hungry, all tired. Let's ask our host to take care of our bodily needs—now."

The tone of the assemblage changed entirely and any shouts or remarks were in agreement with what Donley had told them. And Apdar, with a nod of approval, rose to the occasion.

"Your leader speaks truth," he said. The word "leader" tickled Randall. Amazed Donley. "Apdar will continue later on with discussion. We now go below to sleep quarters and eating place. You will all be provided with the necessities until—" Thinking better of what he was about to conclude with, he left it hang in the air.

As they filed out of the hall in the wake of their host, they were a quieted and thoughtful group. Some whispered of experiencing the feel of the pulsation,

56

others said they had not felt it. Still others spoke hopelessly of the implications of disaster to come. But of all those in the company, the two girls with their new-found boyfriends—not to speak of the honeymoon couples—were least concerned of all. And Donley was thinking more of Mera than of anything else. He fell in step with Apdar, who was leading his guests to a wide double door at the side of the rotunda.

"I'd like most of all to see the living-dead from the *Saturnia*," he declared, as they passed through and started down a long ramp.

Apdar gazed at him kindly. "You hope to see somebody you know?"

"Someone I love."

"Oh! I take you as soon as sleep rooms assigned."

Donley could barely hold back his impatience any longer. As they descended toward a lower level of the dome, he was acutely aware of the beat in his mind and body.

Lub-dub, lub-dub, lub-dub.

CHAPTER EIGHT

The level below presented a maze of connecting corridors with many adjacent doors set in their metal walls, on the order of a Terran hotel. One after another of the visitors was assigned quarters by Apdar and these proved to be spacious and comfortably furnished. Air-conditioned to a temperature and relative humidity that would surely suit the majority of them, besides which each room had its own controls. The illumination was flush, similar to fluorescent, soft and ample, as bright as the sunlight of Mars and the color of that of Terra. The Underwoods and the Carters found themselves in suites consisting of sitting room, bedroom and bath, in much the tradition of hotel accommodations to which they were accustomed on the solar system planets. Donley and Randall located in adjoining rooms and then the audio system carried Apdar's voice to all, summoning them to their first meal on Ormin.

Apdar bent his head to Donley's whisper: "I can't eat yet. Not until I find the girl. Won't you take me to the *Saturnia* survivors?"

Most of the others were now gathering to accept the invitation to eat and their host was occupied for a few minutes getting them in line to enter the automatic cafeteria-type dining room nearby. Randall was fidgeting also—but for a different reason.

Apdar showed the way while Randall trailed along

and started a conversation with Apdar that was a bit too technical for Donley to follow with his mind in its present state regarding Mera. In fact, his impatience was now so great that he found it difficult to keep mum. Had he been of a less tolerant mold he would have voiced objection in no uncertain terms.

Apdar sensed his uneasiness for he interrupted Randall and said to Donley, "Past next corner we come to your way down. Very quick now."

They came then into another corridor where there was an offset in which appeared an installation with handrails and down-sloping steps that was certainly an escalator. Apdar touched a button and the moving stair began its downward glide, smoothly and silently.

"Everything automated here, Apdar?" breathed Randall.

"Must be, friend, or I not be here alone and alive. Power generation, food production, everything necessary, needs no attendant." He then turned again to Donley. "Down this and following ones you come to next level, then next and next. In each are living-dead. In third are those from previous ship. Good luck, my friend."

Donley found the gliding movement of the escalator too slow and he skittered down the first one, two steps at a time. Turned a corner and stepped on the succeeding one but not before he had seen, in an eerie low-level lighting, a huge area where lay rows of bodies that did not move. Some laid out carefully, others in the uncomfortable position in which they had dropped. In suspended animation. The living-dead. The next level was much the same, excepting that a few of the bodies were laid out in caskets. They must have run out of coffins at a later time. The third level down was a really solemn place, with row upon row of caskets of the drop-side type, in each of which lay one of the living-dead. Here he would find Mera, Donley's heart told him.

In the nearest of the caskets lay a man of stalwart build, a compatriot of Apdar, Donley was sure. His features were acquiline, his brow wide and high beneath a mop of curley black hair. The expression on his face was serene and his hands were crossed on his breast. His skin was cool to the touch, but not cold. This was not death; Apdar had aptly described the state of suspended animation as "living-death."

From bier to bier Donley now shuttled. Here and there were women, some young, some old, some fair, some plain. Their garments were of unfamilar style, not of Terra, Venus, or Mars. The next long row included a few closed caskets; actual death had struck here, Donley realized. Quite likely natural death. Conscious of the pulse that came monotonously through the faintly discernible whine of distant machinery, though not as a sound, Donley went swiftly along this row and still found only those covered with the unfamiliar garments of Ormin. His breath was coming short from nerve strain and exertion, though the cool, circulating air would have been a tonic under ordinary conditions.

What if he had been wrong? What if Mera were not here? Worse yet, what if she *were* here but in one of the closed caskets? It was a ghastly place, he decided. Like a huge open catacomb but even more fearsome because of the sense of possible sudden reviving, or at least movement of one or more of the corpses that were not corpses. Especially it seemed that way after he had viewed a number of young people, both male and female, who were beautiful to see and so natural in repose that he imagined several times he had seen the rise and fall of a chest, the move of a hand.

And then he came to a man who was clothed in the habiliments of New York or Chicago. A husky American business man, with the hint of a smile on his lips and appearing as if about to rise up and walk. In the next open casket was a beautiful bronze-skinned Martian woman, also seeming about to come fully alive. Donley scurried along from one to another, his heart now pounding with excitement since these were without doubt survivors of the *Saturnia*. Another closed casket and his heart skipped a beat. Then a dream girl, yes—*his* dream girl. It must be; it was—Meral

The curtain had best be drawn on the scene that immediately ensued. Stronger men than Jack had broken down in circumstances less emotionally charged.

Eventually he came to realize that he had lifted the girl partially and was cuddling her head and upper body in his arms. She hadn't changed much, in fact not at all excepting that her lips did not respond to his own. And they were cold. Not really cold but cool. He guessed wildly that her body temperature was at least twenty degrees below normal. Returning her to the position in which she had lain, he folded the slim hands over her breasts as they had been. There was only a slight stiffness of the idle joints, certainly no rigor mortis. He stroked her soft brown hair with shaking fingers. She was alive but unaware. However, the time would come for her to return to awareness and her former youthful vigor and ebullience. Donley knew that this was so, regardless of Apdar's gloomy predictions. He just *knew* it.

Fighting off the feeling that she had moved slightly,

61

he turned away and stumbled blindly along the aisle, suddenly overcome with nameless terror. Every bier held lurking shadows of things that moved or were about to move. The air of the huge golgotha seemed stifling and suddenly filled with whisperings of words better left unsaid.

Through it all, and pressing down on him was the endless rhythm. *Lub-dub, lub-dub, lub-dub*. Modifying the faint hum of distant machines.

At the foot of the up escalator, he shook his head to clear it.

He had no pangs of hunger, nor did he yearn for sleep so he went up to the floor of the dome, looking for Randall and Apdar. He recalled a few words of what Randall had been saying and was sure the two would be in a laboratory or observatory of Apdar's. But where was it? The first four doors he tried were locked, then the fifth opened into a passage that led to a circular stair. Donley bounded up this until he became dizzy and eventually found himself near the dome's top. Here there was a solid floor against which the stairway ended. Looking for signs of a trap door, he located the line of closure with the ceiling and a curiously shaped handle which he was just able to reach. But the handle couldn't be turned; the entrance to the room above was locked. That Randall and Apdar were up there, deep in studies of the heavens, he had not the slightest doubt. In fact he distinctly heard movement up there and the song of a variable speed motor such as is used to move a telescope mounting. Well, if they wanted privacy, he supposed that was their privilege and rightly so. They were the scientists, not he.

Back on the dome floor, he saw Jal Tarjen crossing to one of the doors he had previously tried.

"It's locked, Jal."

Startled, the Martian turned and a smile wreathed his face at sight of Donley. "So you feel wakeful, also," he offered, crossing over. "And you did not eat?"

"Didn't feel like eating," Donley told him. "But I've seen some of the region below the living quarters. Like to see more. What say we go together."

"Nothing better to do. Most everybody asleep in own rooms. Tired. I found library but can not read language. So we go; good idea."

Using the down escalators, the two visited the halls of the living-dead. It was unexpectedly depressing to the Martian, judging from his silence and grim set of his features. At length—Donley was unable to resist seeing her again—they came to the resting place of Mera. Donley had himself in hand now and stroked the soft hair with steady fingers, then bent down and kissed the cool lips.

"This your lady?" Tarjen asked softly.

"Yes. See why I didn't feel like eating?"

"I see why, yes." The Martian's voice rose slightly. "She can't be on way to destruction like they say. Too lovely. You need her too much, Donley."

"Jal Tarjen, you're a pal. I agree all the way."

Somehow the Martian's words had inspired Donley. Like restoring his courage and faith. He patted Mera's hand, leaned over and kissed her once more. "See you later," he whispered in her ear. And he believed he would—implicitly.

Straightening up, he gripped Jal's hand. "Let's see more of this place," he said. "There's got to be lots more."

At the end of the huge chamber opposite the escalators, he thought he saw an arched opening leading into a passage. It turned out to be the entrance to a ramp that curved downward. The lighting here was even more somber than in the upper levels and when they reached the bottom of the ramp they stepped warily into another chamber that was the terminal of a gravity lift. Without hesitation, they entered the lift and were dropped smoothly and swiftly in darkness for what seemed like perhaps fifty feet. The lift stopped and a door opened automatically into another huge repository of the living-dead. The Martian sort of groaned in his throat.

"I know," said Donley. "Spooky, isn't it?"

The light was dimmer here than anywhere they had been and there were longer aisles of coffins and more of them. These were open also but not drop-side. Only from the waist up could the occupants be seen. All appeared to be countrymen of Apdar's, with wives and children—row after row as far as you could see into the gloom.

Jal Tarjen whistled softly between his teeth, a habit he had when disturbed. "Must be thousands," he muttered. "At least three—here," Donley agreed. "These must have been among the earliest to succumb. They ran out of coffins later."

"What was that?" the Martian husked.

"What was what?"

"Blue light—moving. There, again."

And then Jack saw it too. An eerie blue glow moving between the rows of coffins several aisles from them, bobbing rhythmically up and down, as if carried by a creature that walked. Fleetingly, it came to Donley that its movements coincided with the lub-dub of the pulse.

But he shook off the thought—there was enough without that.

"Who's there?" he called out.

There was no reply but the light, whatever it was, flicked off. Donley was sure he could see a shadowy form slithering away from where the light had been. He bent forward to see better in the gloom and his hand brushed the face of a corpse that was not a corpse but felt like one. He shuddered involuntarily at the contact, the face being cold and clammy, yes colder than was Mera's skin to the touch. Must be the time element, he thought. He then peered closely into the face and was rewarded by seeing in calm repose the features of a most beautiful girl, a blonde child of perhaps eight years. If ages ran the same here as on earth. He shuddered anew at the thought that—but, she would not die. None of them would. This phase was a bad dream. Destruction of all of these and of themselves? Nuts!

Jal Tarjen, a few feet away, called out in a Martian dialect that was unintelligible to Jack.

There was a quick reply in the same tongue and a twisted, wrinkled ancient from the Martian drylands hobbled, slowly and painfully, to get on his knees before Jal Tarjen. He looked up into the faces of the two men, seeming to approve of what he saw. Then he spoke rapidly in the outlandish tongue for several minutes, addressing himself to Tarjen. His watery old eyes blinked in their crinkled setting as he finished and he rose creakingly to his feet.

Amazement was written large on Jal Tarjen's face as he turned to Donley. "Man says he sent by queen from other realm to bring us there. This place deeper down and many vanirs to west but he guides us to the

65

one who want to see us. Says this unknown to Apdar, another race once enemies. East against them and they against east long time back. She know about us, about Apdar, about living death. But say no effect of pulsation in her domain. This hard to believe, Donley."

Understanding not a word, the distorted old drylander looked into Donley's eyes as if to confirm what he had told Jal. And the American could not but believe that what he saw in the lined and weathered old face and faded eyes was complete honesty.

"Must be so," said Donley. "Anyway, what can we lose? Let's go."

Tarjen translated rapidly to his gnomish compatriot and the little drylander shuffled swiftly off down the aisle, looking back to see if they were following. They were. And it was amazing the speed with which the ancient could step along. His blue light was again on and it cast weird flickering shadows of the numberless sarcophagi on walls and ceiling. Donley was not sorry to be leaving.

At length they came to a gravity lift shaft, the door to which was cleverly concealed in the frescoes of an ornamental or ceremonial niche of the metal wall at the far end of the chamber. They were dropped for what seemed an endless distance into the bowels of the planet, then came out in a tunnel where a monorail car awaited them. A ten-seater.

Cocking his head to one side and closing his eyes to concentrate, Donley could discern no hint of the stellar beat in his consciousness.

The car whisked them off into the blackness of the tunnel with effortless acceleration. Whatever its motive power might be, it was as silent as it was mighty, for their backs pressed into the seats as in the blast-off of an ethership.

CHAPTER NINE

As the tunnel car sped through the smooth-walled tube at a velocity he judged to be just under that of sound, Donley turned over in his mind some of the implications of what he had just heard. East against West. West against East. Two ideologies, two ways of life, two groups of nations or of States, with suspicions and enmities mounting to unreasonable proportions over a period of time. Until the inevitable happened. Whether one was the agressor group and the other defensive made little difference in the parallel to what had been going on for a century or more on his own world. Each side had built up a huge arsenal of nuclear devices here in Ormin and eventually, whether by accident or design, had triggered off the exchange of searing blasts which had devastated the planet and destroyed its civilizations. That each side had been able to burrow in with a few survivors and develop a new civilization of its own was something to contemplate.

Jal Tarjen and the drylander had been conversing for what seemed like an interminable time in that guttural dialect, the drylander's weird blue light making gargoyles of their faces and casting grotesque shadows of them on the swiftly receding tunnel walls. Eventually the big Martian began translating to Donley.

"We arrive quite soon," he said. "This place about

67

five hundred and fifty of your miles from the place we left. Just west of terminator on bright side of Ormin. Six vanirs—ten of your miles deep. People come from old enemies of eastern territorials so still keep location secret. Their ruler a woman. Name of Daila. She have mind power that learn much in recent time. Know about living-dead and why. But cause of same does not reach her or her people. She learn of us and send man for us so we can talk."

"Man? You mean the little old guy, of course. How did he get to the place? I don't get it."

"Came from *Saturnia*. Daila also have airlock to surface. They go out, rocket to wreck after Apdar's rescue, find him left behind. Sick. So they bring back and heal. But—"

The speedy tunnel car was slowing down so they must be nearing the end of the ride. By Donley's wrist chronometer they had been less than an hour on the way! Earth time. They came into a lighted stretch of the tube and finally to a platform where the car came smoothly to rest. A group of humans, whose uniform attire gave them the appearance of police officers or guards of some sort, awaited them.

Which is exactly what they were, and a fine looking lot. About half were male and the other half female. Bright-faced, smiling, everyone of them. And with the erect postures of soldiery. But with no arms of any kind, not even the billies carried by the police of Risapar, planet Mars.

One who seemed to be their leader stepped out of line and the word "Welcome" came from his smiling countenance. But there was no movement of his lips. This was thought communication. "Will you come with us please? We go to Daila."

There was a feeling of near reverence in the thought-word "Daila."

Standing before her, a little later, Donley could well understand that note of reverence. For here was a woman so unusual, so enchanting, and yet so obviously consecrated to an ideal or ideals and to the welfare of her people as to stand out as beyond compare. Her features were chiseled and serene, her color creamy with just the proper blending of rose in cheeks and lips. Her smile was contagious, her manner imperious yet humble. The crown of taffy blonde hair that waved about her smooth brow completed the impression of saintliness that surrounded her like an aura. Yet her body, as revealed by the closely fitting garment she wore, was flawlessly perfect in form, and enticing. She sat slightly forward in the plainly decorated seat that was on a small platform a foot higher than the main floor of her audience room. Her lips moved excitingly to form words in her own tongue, accompanied by thought images understandable to both Donley and the Martian as a fervent welcome. Daila was a telepathist, they were to learn, as were all of her subjects to lesser degree.

She dismissed the guards and the grinning drylander, thanking them all for what they had done. "Be seated, friends," she conveyed to her two visitors, indicating a cushioned divan that faced her only a few feet away.

Donley and the Martian sank into the cushions, both enslaved. Donley thought grimly how right Tarjen had been when he told him he needed Mera "too much." He wondered if this vision should be addressed as "majesty."

Reading the thought, she smiled: "I am Daila and

no more. Think of me, speak of me in that term." Then she came to the point. "I sent for you because I seek your help in what is about to transpire. I'll explain as well as I can. We here are about four thousand in number, selectively bred in the line descending from the small group of escapees from the great war of annihilation, escapees from the powerful western alliance. Your vessel of space was brought down near a similar refuge, that of those descended from our ancient enemy, the equally powerful eastern territorial alliance. We here have long since forgotten all past hatreds and bitterness but are not sure the same can be said of the easterners. Especially since all of them but Apdar now lie in suspended animation."

"You—you know all about that?" gasped Donley. "How?"

Daila smiled her enchanting smile. "Just say for the moment that I'm clairvoyant, though that is not the correct designation for the gift that is mine. Suffice it to say that we know all about what has been determined by Apdar, and now your own scientist—by purely material technology. We know of the pulsation Apdar claimed was of his making, of the anticipated destruction of our planet Ormin by collision with another body from out of space. But our picture of that event does not admit of despair, only of faith in survival, and in a new life that is not yet clearly envisioned. One doubt that does remain is that there may still be the easterners to reckon with. We do not want nor are we prepared for another period of warfare. And that is where you two come in; we have great hopes that you may act as mediators or at least learn for our information what the likelihood is of our peaceful existence in the same environment as the easterners.

Jal Tarjen exclaimed delightedly. Donley's heart

leaped with renewal of his own flagging hopes. "You really think we'll come through this collision in space?" he asked.

"So far as I can now determine, I do. But more of this later. I had almost forgotten an event of interest to you. There was a small ship of space, an auxiliary of your larger vessel, that landed devoid of fuel, in the ravine where our airlock above is hidden. We took in the three men who were aboard but now have them under restraint. They shot and killed one of my subjects who was assisting in their rescue. This is another of my reasons for bringing you here."

"It's very important," Donley averred, "to us and to you. And to World Space Authority, I'm sure. May we see the prisoners?"

"Certainly. I had hoped you would wish to do so."

She touched a flush wall plate and immediately there entered a small detachment of three guards. "They will conduct you," she advised, "and return you here for the remainder of our talk."

They were taken out onto a balcony which looked over a deep well that was girded by tier after tier of similar balconies, teaming with life in some cases. From down there came the throb of machinery and a transparent-walled lift cage rose up from the depths to their level. One of the guards indicated that they would use this and the five stepped inside. The lift was, by intent it appeared, slow in descent, so that they were able to look into some of the workings of Daila's inner realm.

There were a number of the balconies from which corridors led off into what were obviously living quarters similar to those beneath the dome of Apdar. Another balcony opened into wide spaces of park-like

71

appearance where growing things bloomed in profusion, floral and vegetable, in regular arrangement and with men and women working in several areas. A light rain of water was misting over one side, artificial sunlight bathed the other. Here was utility and beauty combined.

Another level opened out from a balcony, revealing vistas of manufacturing machines. Textiles, art materials, hard goods of all kinds, electronic equipment, minor repair work, all could be made here either on a quantity production or small job manufacturing basis.

Still another balcony opened into recreation areas, where games of various sorts seemed to be in progress. If time had only permitted, this would have been meat for Donley. As it was, it brought back memories of the Interplan contests he had competed in, not too many years back.

Near the lowest level of all were the utilities, nuclear power generators, oxygen equipment, refrigeration, humidity control, huge blowers and their plenums from which ductwork branched off in all directions to carry the manufactured atmosphere. This miscellany of rotating machinery gave fourth a variation of not unmusical tones, with heterodyne beats between frequencies that differed from one another.

The lift stopped and they stepped onto a moving way to a pokey such as he had once visited in a lunar prison. The three were in separate cells, Captain Stark pacing the narrow confines of his, the other two sitting on their cots, sullen and defiant. The Martian recognized these two at once.

"Why," he exclaimed, "these men are from the *Phobos*. Plenty bad! Plenty bad!"

One of them spat at him through the bars. Donley stopped at Captain Stark's cell and was greeted with a

72

torrent of words. The captain swore the other two had forced him with a gun at his back to take them away in the escape ship, that he had knocked out the steward to save his life as the stowaways had planned to kill him as they had the two crew members they were then impersonating. He said he jettisoned most of the auxiliary's fuel, and asked for a chance to tell his story to Randall and the mate, assuming that both had survived the crash of the *Meteoric*, which he had witnessed from afar.

"They did; we all survived," Donley told the quaking, mustache-chewing prisoner. "But how come these crooks stowed away on the *Meteoric* in the first place? Just to escape the law on Terra?"

"That, and to make a getaway with some contraband they carried on board. In a steel box, whatever it is."

"Ya-ah!" croaked the beetle-browed thug in the next cell. "You'll never know what it is. And you're in this as deep as we are, you rat!"

Amazingly, the captain held his temper. Instead of raging at the man, he continued his pleading with Donley to intervene for him. Inclined to believe his story, Donley promised he would do what he could, but explained the situation that would probably make his intercession too late, with so short a time remaining until the predicted collision.

The captain paled at the news but threw back his shoulders. "If that happens we'll all go together—and never know what hit us. But I'd like them to *know* anyway—before—"

"I can do that much at least," Donley promised. "Tell them."

"Thanks. And I had nothing to do with the killing here, either. That louse in the second cell did it."

73

"Rat!" came from that quarter. "Anyway—prove it!"

Donley glanced at his timepiece. "We'll have to hurry back, Captain. Time's getting short." He just barely touched his chin.

Stark clung to his bars as they left and Donley didn't want to look back. There was too much of the whipped dog in the once self-sufficient and arrogant ship's master.

"Well?" Dalia's thought questioned them when they had returned.

"Bad, bad men—the two," Tarjen ejaculated, then bent his massive head toward Donley to indicate him as spokesman.

"The other," he told Daila, "was captain of the *Meteoric*. And I believe his story that he was forced to take the smugglers in the small rocket job. But they all spoke of a metal box—"

"We have it," Daila smiled, "and have not opened it. Would you like to see its contents?"

"Not now. Nor do we want any of the prisoners—yet. I grant you have first claim on them here. One of your own was killed, besides which time is short and the future too uncertain—as far as I'm concerned." Donley wished fervently he could feel more of Daila's trust. "I would discuss it with Apdar and our scientist anyway before acting."

"This I approve. Even if you must wait until after the collision."

Jack stared. She had expressed knowledge of this before, of the anticipated collision. But here was assurance that she definitely felt they would all be here after the fact.

"How can you be so sure we'll live through it?" he

inquired, hoping from her reply to regain some of his own previous assurance, especially with respect to Mera.

Daila's countenance shone with a look of dedication. "We have clung to the beliefs of our ancestors and these included the premise of the ultimate triumph of good and the doctrine of faith in the future rather than in ultimate doom. Much of it is legendary, but our forefathers we know were far happier in their beliefs than the easterners had been in their political ideologies and devotion to the material sciences as above all other ologies in importance. Actually, we have developed sciences such as cosmology and ontology to a degree now approaching perfection. This is in contrast to the entirely material technology of Adpar—and I take it of most of your own people. To begin with, our concept of the universe is that it was created by a master mind or intelligence and is still controlled by this power. We think of the cosmos as a colossal organism with life and percipience like a human being. With comparable voluntary and involuntary functions. Just as the natural functioning of human body mechanisms produces antibodies to combat disease germs, or healing fluids that are sent to the site of an injury such as lymph for the coagulation of blood, we believe that this sentient cosmos is now in the process of healing the sore spot in its midst that was Ormin—"

Donley stared, interrupting her thought train. "You sure you've not been probing Doctor Randall's mind?" he asked.

"Doctor Randall, your scientific man? No, not more than superficially to learn his main interests. Why?"

"Randall has expressed beliefs very similar to those you just now expounded. With the exception of the

75

very last thought, the healing of a lost planet. It's astonishing."

"Not to me. He is apparently a deep thinker in addition to being a student of the material sciences and an agent of your space authority. Naturally, a man like this would gravitate to what we know is Truth. He simply could not, in the end, deny the existence of a Plan and that an infinite intelligence is behind it all."

"How do you explain the pulsation that has been so powerful in its effects? The bringing of madness and of a coma on board our ethership. The living-death in the realm of Adpar?"

"It is as yet unexplained, insofar as its source and how it produces these effects is concerned. If indeed in the region of the dome it is the identical beat as that in your vessel. Quite likely it is this throb that causes the living-death in the easterners and the reason it does not reach us here is our depth within the planet and the layers of insulating material in the crust above us, such as metallic ores. Here, you see, is where the physical and metaphysical overlap where it is sometimes most difficult to resolve the problem. Eventually, we shall know the truth of this still unexplained phenomenon."

"But you're convinced that all the so-called living-dead in Adpar's diggings will survive?" Donley hung anxiously on her reply.

"Indeed we are. And that they will awaken to a much better world in which to live a far better life. At the moment, our strongest wish is that a lasting peace will prevail between east and west when Ormin is rejuvenated."

"I sure hope you're right." Donley told her. "You

see, I have one I love back there. She's in that state and it's for her I'm concerned."

Daila's understanding permeated her thought-words. "I know," she said. "Not in detail but I have known of your great love and concern. May I offer our shelter here, my friend? Bring your Mera here before the cataclysm. She will be safe, I assure you. The time is short, so you had best return at once. And here is a means of communicating with me." She handed him a shiny metal instrument the size of a cigaret case. It was smooth on all sides save one and here there was a series of six or seven small buttons that projected a quarter inch from the side.

"You press the buttons in this sequence," Daila instructed him. "*Two, five, one, three.* Then merely talk into the flat side. Use it, my friend, in any circumstance where you think it may be useful. I shall do anything within my power that you may ask—to help."

She had pressed the wall plate and a contingent of her guards stood before them. "Go now," she continued. "And please do what you can for us when the time comes. If you can get an answer before the impending collision, just use the communicator and let me know. Farewell, but not for long."

Donley and the Martian, impelled by an urge they could not have explained, each bent and kissed one of the soft hands, then turned away to follow their guides.

Somehow, though the passage was well-lighted, they seemed engulfed in a deepening gloom once they had passed through the portals.

CHAPTER TEN

After escorting them to the tunnel car, Daila's guards offered to go along with them but Donley and the Martian agreed that this was not necessary. If they couldn't retrace so simple a route they had poor memories indeed. One last bit of advice from the head guard was to take the gravity lift to its termination, which was a few levels higher than where they had entered it with the drylander. In that way there would be no need for manual control of the lift and they would see other areas of the domain of the easterners.

It was the best advice they could have received, Donley thought as they stepped out of the concealed niche into which the lift shaft opened at the top of its travel. Not only had they missed the not too cheerful repositories of the corpses that were not corpses, they were in the hub of the easterners' habitation. Where the various automated services essential to their continued existence and growth over the years were located. In contrast to the balconied arrangement of its western counterpart, the domain of Adpar was divided into separate chambers of varying size and usefulness. Instead of a level where at least a portion of the westerners' diet was raised and a separate level for utilities and still another for manufacturing, all three functions were combined here in one huge domed interior. The sounds of rotating machinery were very much the same, but otherwise there was not too much in common between the two concepts. However, there were here illustrated some of the fundamental differences between east and west.

Food production was all by machines; there was no area where the inhabitants, before the living-death, could have raised fresh vegetables for dietary purposes or flowers for their beauty and aroma. Their food, however appetizing, was all ersatz. Manufacturing areas had been set up by the easterners on a strictly quantity production basis and the units making up the utilities were of massive construction, that is the individual pieces of equipment, generators, pumps, blowers and such, were bulky and strictly functional in design, not streamlined for space and weight saving in addition to appearance, as were those in Daila's realm.

There simply must be a separate chamber for physical fitness and recreational programs. There was, as they discovered upon leaving the ramp they took upward from the far end of this area. They came into a completely equipped gymnasium that was alongside a game room, both of huge size and equal or superior to corresponding facilities provided in the west.

Casting about for a means of reaching the dome room, they came upon another gravity lift, this one of course provided with the type of call button used in Adpar's diggings. The door opened at Donley's touch and they managed to get inside before it closed upon them. There was only one up button so they had no choice. They found themselves on the floor of the rotunda when they stepped out.

An unexpected sight greeted them. Over at the open door to the circular stair well, Randall was bending over the still form of Apdar, straightening his legs.

He then crossed the man's hands over his chest and rose to face Donley and the Martian.

"Yes," he said slowly, "it finally got to him. His living-death."

It was then that Donley noticed the pendant hanging from the slim chain that encircled Randall's neck, a duplicate of the one worn by Adpar.

"What's the decoration, Randall?" he asked lightly.

His question was evaded. Instead of answering it, Randall mumbled, "Much more work to be done topside." And before Donley could do more than gape, he was up the circular stair to the observatory.

Donley would have followed him expecting for the fact that Lantag strolled in with the news that most of the *Meteoric's* passengers and all but one of the crew had succumbed. Most of these, he said, had never left their beds since first getting into them. The newlyweds, both couples, were among the living-dead, as well as the two young girls Eula and Byrl, also Brand and Davidson. Apparently, the few of them remaining up and around were of hardier stock, or with differently constituted nervous systems, to resist the thing longer. But, even as Lantag was telling them these things, Donley could feel the measured pulse of the energy stream in his consciousness. He shook his head to clear it just as Mr. Standish came in to join them.

"What do we hear from up there?" he asked, indicating the top of the dome with a toss of his head. "They've been locked in for—" He saw the motionless body of Adpar. "—hours, without a word. Ah, I see our benefactor has had it," he concluded.

"Yes," Donley replied, "and I imagine we'll follow in short order."

It was then that Randall's voice came to them from

the audios. It was in calm and measured tones that he requested all who heard him to get together in the amphitheatre. "I want to do a little explaining," he said, "and show you on the screen what we, that is Adpar and myself, determined before he slipped away."

Jal Tarjen said then, "All will hear this. A speaker is in every room, every corridor, All over."

They moved toward the small bowl and soon there were seated in a row half-way back, eight of them in all. Two of these were from the crew of the *Meteoric* but the steward was not with them. There was one woman, a square-jawed amazon type, a tall beanpole of a man with thick spectacles, a stout oldster with thinning gray hair, Lantag, Jal Tarjen and Donley. With Doc in the observatory, this meant that nineteen of their number were in suspended animation.

Donley did a quick double-take, made sure the mate was not with them, then rushed outside. Sure enough, Mr. Standish had dropped in a heap, just before reaching the double doors, and all that Jack could do for him was to compose his arms and legs as Randall had done with Adpar. Time was running out!

A screen not too unlike the large optophone disc in the main saloon of the *Meteoric* lighted a moment after Donley resumed his seat and Randall began telling them about what he was ready to show. His features and the sag of his shoulders betrayed extreme weariness.

"Before I run any cinetape," he said, "I'd better give you a brief rundown on some of the past of Ormin. Like Terra, there were years of preparation for nuclear defense and, strangely, this was between east and west as in our own case. Eventually came the horror of nuclear war on a world scale and, according to history tape which Apdar showed me, all habitable and uninhabitable areas of the surface were devastated and all of the populations destroyed with the exception of a few of the eastern territorials who escaped the holocaust by being in a previously prepared underground shelter.

"There were no pictures at this time but only words on the tape, so we have to rely on oral description. I'll not bore you with all of it but it seems there were four men and four women, with two young children of one couple, and from these descended the five thousand who inhabitated this city as of the coming of the living-death. The city itself was a result of gradual growth over the years, five of the fugitives being engineers of one persuasion or another, working with and educating their offspring in the beginning. They mined their ores, smelted them, forged and machined required finished members as they expanded their quarters and multiplied in number. Power generation, water supply, oxygen and other gas production of their simulated atmosphere, refrigeration, food processing—all had to be expanded in capacity from time to time as the population grew. Generation after generation built up the city and its facilities.

"The planet Ormin, for reasons that are unclear, gradually slowed its rotation until one side always faced Sirius, its sun. Poisoned by radioactivity and fallout, its atmosphere changed composition in a slow mutation that expanded the altered gases and consumed the oxygen, leaving behind only the most tenuous gases and these soon left the gravitational field of the planet entirely. Fortunately, the airlock which had protected them against the poisoned gases proved

82

equally effective against the now surrounding vacuum. The transparent dome and its later designed outer airlock were of comparatively recent construction, having been conceived and built by Apdar's grandfather, who was then the leader of the easterners."

Since much of this, excepting the portions referring only to the easterners, was already familiar to Donley, he had been spending most of his energy watching in the dim light the row of seats for signs of others succumbing to the energy beat. And so it was that he saw one of the crewmen topple forward and hang limply against the seat in front of him. It was Lantag who helped him carry the man to the rotunda and lay him out beside the mate. The woman next in the row let out with a long fluttering sigh as they lifted the man over her head. She wasn't feeling too good, Donley thought.

For that matter, neither was he. The sensation of the beating pulse was strong in his brain and he needed quite a bit of head-shaking and self-discipline to clear it of the *lub-dub, lub-dub, lub-dub's* potency.

However, when they came back to their seats and he saw that Randall was running a cinetape, he felt better.

"This tape," Randall explained, "was pieced together over the years and all portions of it were taken here in the city. Naturally, the first footage is not too good, showing the wear of many runnings. There were not more than five hundred inhabitants when the first portion was made."

What he had said was true; the tape showed horizontal streaks and snow on the screen to an extent that almost made some of it unrecognizable. But it showed mostly all of the five hundred easterners gathered in a large hall which evidently had been replaced since. They were in seats part of the time, milling about in the aisles from time to time and shouting unintelligible objections to what the speaker was telling them in the same language. Frequently, their shouted hecklings drowned out the man's voice entirely. It was obvious that a state of great excitement prevailed, even of fear.

"Apdar interpreted this to me," Randall stated. "It was at the time Ormin was hurled from its orbit by an undetermined force, making it a wanderer in space. The man addressing them, or trying to, was the chief scientist of that time and he was telling them what was about to occur. Some didn't believe him, others believing and overcome with terror. A scene of confusion like this was bound to ensue. Watch now!"

The floor of the hall rocked and the humans were tossed hither and yon as if an earthquake of enormous strength was shaking their entire city, or perhaps refuge is the better word as it had hardly become a city at that period. There were screams and stampeding and certainly many of the participants must have lost their lives as they fell or were shoved to fall under the feet of the crowd. Ormin was out of its orbit!

"Not too many lost their lives," Randall averred. "Apdar said history recorded only about fifteen, which is remarkable considering what we have just seen." The view in the screen blanked out and was replaced.

There followed a few scenes in various portions of the growing city as it was expanded, taken during succeeding generations. Interesting records of the diligence with which the growing population added to the facilities of their underground retreat. They were making it a world within a world that was unliveable on its surface.

Then came a section of the tape that gave evidence

of being recently made. "Apdar had most of the rest of this recorded," said Randall. "In the beginning here you see a view through his optical scanner when he first learned that a mysterious energy had taken hold of Ormin and was sweeping it in a huge arc across the heavens in the direction of our solar system. From then on, he studied its course assiduously."

A view of the heavens showed our sun as a bright star and a few of its planets could be made out with comparative ease. From the slow swing of the view it was evident that the instrument picturing it was traveling in a curved path. Whether this was orbital with reference to some other celestial body or bodies was not apparent, but these were the determinations which Apdar had then set out to make.

The view changed to show the inside of Apdar's operating room, the identical one where he had operated on the injured *Meteoric* passenger. A young woman was on the table, covered with a sheet, apparently dead. But Apdar was going over her with care, using first a stethoscope then instruments unfamiliar to Donley. One must have been of the order of an oscilloscope because electrodes from it, when attached to various parts of the woman's body, activated a pen-drawing device at the same time a wavy horizontal line flickered in a round window on its face. The line, whether viewed in the window or on the unrolling paper under the pen, showed a definite cyclic series of notches. In pairs, one notch larger than its mate. Like the lub-dub rhythm. Which it was—precisely.

Apdar looked up with wonder in the eyes above his mask. "She is not dead," Doc translated his words, "but is in a state of suspended animation. There is no heart beat nor is she breathing. But her body temperature is not down to the point indicating death. Nor is there any sign of rigor mortis setting in."

He was telling this to three white-robed and masked assistants at the table. Donley thought he saw a look of cunning come into his eyes as he continued: "It is as I hoped for, why I developed the cause. A period of irrationality, followed by this." He pointed dramatically to the still form under the sheet. "So that we shall all be asleep when Ormin is destroyed." His listeners reacted with violent surprise; this was obviously the first they had heard of this.

Continuing on and on, the tape now showed how one after another and sometimes in groups, Apdar's people succumbed. Some were in a frenzy first, some in babbling lunacy, others joined the living-dead with no preceding mental effect. Casket makers were shown at work and the filling of the lowest level into which Donley and the Martian had ventured, then the level above. Always the ranks of the workers were thinning and by the time the next higher level was filled with living-dead in their drop-side caskets, there were no more manufactured. The few remaining workers must perforce turn to other tasks necessary to sustain the rapidly diminishing population. Eventually, all were of the living-dead, Apdar being the last to survive.

"And so he continued his study of the situation with his excellent astronomical gear," Randall faltered, "and—and I worked with him of late. Now he too has slipped into the state he called the living-death."

Donley closed his eyes and immediately the *lub-dub, lub-dub* pulse was in his being, growing now in intensity. Terrifying, yet soothing. Resolutely, he opened his eyes and set himself against it, determinedly turning his thought to other matters.

He saw suddenly on the wall an audio pickup panel.

Walking down and touching what seemed to be its "talk" button, he said into the mouthpiece, "Can you hear me, Randall?"

"Yes, Donley" came from the several speakers in the small hall. "Go ahead."

Donley hesitated a moment, not knowing if he should smudge Apdar's memory or not. But, for the sake of the rest of them in the seats, he decided he must. "How did our friend get the idea that he had provided the force for the living-death thing? Did he really believe this?"

"Probably not, Donley," Randall laughed. "My guess is that the poor guy was affected mentally a bit himself. Like we've heard of some kooks on earth thinking they're the emperor of Venus."

Emperor of Venus. Creator of the pulsation. What was the difference, as long as one believed it?

Or *had* Apdar believed this? Randall had said not. And Daila had used the word "claimed" in connection with it. Donley would have bet that she knew all of the truth about the harmless conceit.

"Anyway," Randall was saying, "that cinetape brings us up to the time I started working with Apdar. Watch what follows."

CHAPTER ELEVEN

Randall appeared briefly on the screen, scratched his bald pate, then started off in his best lecture-room manner. His image faded and merged into another and clearer view of the starry heavens.

"This is not on tape but is an actual view you are seeing through the telescope up here," he announced. "In the upper right area of the screen you will observe an extremely bright star, which is Sirius. The pale blue ribbon of light that originates near Sirius and arches to the center of the screen, which is our position and point of view, is the energy stream that carries Ormin, and, I believe, the measured beat we have encountered, both here and aboard the *Meteoric*. The selfsame energy stream which carried our ship here willy-nilly. It is now propelling Ormin to its tryst with another heavenly body that is being carried toward the meeting place by a similar beam of energy which comes from a direction almost directly opposite—from the vicinity of our solar system. The other ribbon of energy is reddish of hue but can not now be seen because the other body is so near to us as to block the view. I checked and rechecked Apdar's computations, which show that the two bodies will meet in forty-six minutes, fifteen seconds—as of a few minutes ago when the second check was completed.

"The two are of about the same physical size but

the mass or weight of the other body is amazingly less than a tenth that of Ormin."

The scene now swept dizzily across the screen during the time it required to bring in a closeup of the lightweight planet. At close range, for it was very near indeed, its appearance was that of a spinning orb showing bands of horizontally alternating luminescence and darkness. These belts varied in width from pole to pole and Randall opined that they could only be gaseous in nature. He added that he was now about to receive from the computer the resultant angle and velocity of the two forces carrying the orbs. This would determine their course and destination following the impact.

How calmly Randall envisioned it all! How glibly and unconcernedly he spoke in terms of mathematics and the remaining time. But Donley could see that this planet of doom was drawing nearer by the second; its alternate bands widened as you watched. And then he saw Lantag had slid to the floor and was living-dead already. Others in the row of seat's, five now beside himself, were getting panicky, rising up to start for who knew where. Donley remembered suddenly and confusingly, Mera. Less than forty-five minutes now. He must get to her and take her to Daila!

But the pulse was getting to him. *Lub-dub, lub-dub, lub-dub.* Insistently, Maddeningly. But Mera's only chance, he was certain, was to get to the western city. He fought the beat of the cosmos with all his might, getting Daila's communicator from his pocket awkwardly. Then he flogged his misting brain into recalling the proper sequence in which to press the buttons. His first try brought no response. Must have used the wrong order. *Two, five, six, one, three.* He had it right this time and Daila replied at once, in-

89

structing him swiftly to bring Mera to the level where they had first encountered the drylander. She would have some of her men there to bring him to her with his precious burden. Jal Tarjen was now sagging forward—going—as he left.

Donley had little knowledge of his actions, the throb in his consciousness overpowering everything else. He just wasn't with it, no matter how hard he struggled against the living-death. He *must* get Mera to safety. Must get, must get, must get. A blank space as far as ordinary surroundings were concerned; he drifted into a world of bright fluttering light, blinding him after intermittent plunges into blackness. And then he realized dimly that he had found Mera, that she was in his arms, that he was staggering in search of the hall of the coffins. He never did make it. There were endless vistas of corridors and stairs and ramps, a gravity lift that would only go "up," and always the location of the hall of coffins eluded him. The pulse had him in its grip once more and this time it was not so unpleasant. The beat seemed to be soothing, lulling him to a sense of security and compliance with identical cadence but proclaiming not *lub-dub*, *lub-dub*, *lub-dub* but what registered in his turbulent mind as *let-down*, *let-down*, *let-down*. If only he could let down completely, let the thing take over, nothing else would matter. But here was Mera in his arms, delectable Mera had come through so much to save. *Must* get her to Daila. He managed to recover partly, staggering on, but with mind wandering and senses dulling.

In his growing weakness and confusion, he cried out loudly several times but was answered only by mocking echoes. He had completely forgotten Daila's communicator. The pulse took hold once more and this time it conveyed to him the words *give-up*, *give-*

90

up, give-up. In the end he did just that, slipping easily to his knees, then toppling backward and lying flat with Mera draped across his body.

There came a stupendous jolt, a screaming, roaring crash. Whether it was the prodigious slam of world against world or merely the feeling that accompanied sinking into the living-death, he could never be sure.

At least he had been catapulted into a nirvana of blessed darkness and freedom from cares and fears.

From his point of vantage on the tall seat facing the viewplate of the galactic scanner, the Keeper of Records watched intently as he brought in to closer view a phenomenon not having been duplicated for many aeons past. According to records, that is. Shalag, wraithlike in his gossamer robes and his lined face more deeply furrowed than ever by this concentration, most expert of all scientists of the planet Vloreg, particularly in the fields of galactic astronomy and the programming of computers in celestial mechanics, was intent upon the convergence of two bodies of comparative brightness that bore faint resemblances to comets although not in any sense orbital to any of the major stars of the Milky Way. Although one of the speeding bodies trailed that faint slender tail of barely discernible blue and the other a similar tail of pink. Bringing these into close focus, he saw that the computer was printing out a solution of his previous question. Yes, the two bodies were to collide—at precisely the location designated as 27148_3—9a, 66b, 12c.

Shalag manipulated the controls of the galactic scanner, bringing the speeding bodies into extremely close view. One was obviously a dead world, if indeed it had been populated, the other was a poser for the moment. Of similar size to the first, this apparently was a ball of gases. He fed a tape into the computer after punching it with the request for analysis of these gases. But it was too late for the machine to give him the answer, for already the bodies were almost in contact.

Heavy tides were being raised on the gaseous body as the two neared impact. Then, streamers of what seemed to be flame but was undoubtedly only luminescent gases leaped from the near side of the body toward the other—like the corona of a hot sun when eclipsed by an orbiting planet. Excepting it was on the one side only. Gravity pull.

Shalag blinked his old eyes as these two space wanderers closed in for the rendezvous. He ruminated on the possible causes of it all, his beliefs in the controlling force of a central intelligence telling him that this was a contrived meeting. For what purpose, he could not at the moment conceive. Possibly for the purging of a world contaminated and a menace to some solar system. Shalag had known of such a circumstance within the century.

The blue and red tails, he observed, extended far off into space in almost opposite directions. Quite likely, he ruminated, these were the force streams set up by the central intelligence to carry these two to their fate. Like two arteries in the living organism that was the universe. Arteries that might carry such supplementary palliatives or energies as would be required to effect the desired purging or healing.

Stretching out toward the dead body, the luminescent streamers now licked its surface as they leaped triumphantly from the gaseous orb. And then the two had collided!

The display of pyrotechnics was like nothing Shalag had ever seen in his century of presiding here. Momentarily it was similar to the burst of a nova, with particles thrown off and for the space of a breath outshining the multitude of stars in that area of the firmament. Like fireworks used in some of Vloreg's celebrations. Yet Shalag knew that insufficient heat could be generated in this impact, mighty though it must be, to bring the solid dead body to incandescence. These then were certain of the gases comprising the other body, flammable and explosive. He knew not why but somehow Shalag received the impression that this was all for the good of the dead world. Possibly there was even some form of intelligent life hidden beneath its broken surface.

A single body resulted from the crash, a body that had been without rotation now spinning on its axis and hurtling off at an angle that was the resultant of the two propelling forces toward one of the solar systems. Referring to his chart, Shalag learned that this was the system designated as Vastar 181-x. A quickly taped question brought from his computer the intelligence that this apparently rejuvenated body would orbit with the other plants, in a safe path around Vastar 181-x.

Astonished by his own shaky reaction to the ferocity of the creative encounter he had just witnessed, Shalag took stock of himself and came to the reluctant conclusion that it was time for his successor to be appointed and for him to step down. For he ought not to have been so affected. He reflected that nothing in the universe is born without travail and pain, that no great good is accomplished without some intense hard work and usually many disappointing efforts in advance.

Shalag was aging and should be content to rest on his record.

When consciousness returned to Jack Donley, he opened his eyes with extreme caution, not knowing what they might first see. He lay on his back, blinking in the light of—it couldn't be—yes, it was, the sun! A soft burden, if this could be called a burden, snuggled contentedly on his chest. Mera—at last! He moved her with infinite tenderness so he could sit up, then cradled her head on his knees. Her color was rising with her body temperature and soon there came a flutter of the long lashes. Her incredibly blue eyes opened, took in Donley with a long fond gaze and then, half crying, half laughing, she rose up only sufficiently to reach his lips with her own, to cling to him with desperate abandon. It had been so long!

"Jack, Jack darling. It's really you," she was murmurring as he kissed her neck, her ears, even the tip of her pert nose, then returned to her lips for more of their nectar.

"And it's you!" he marveled. "What I've dreamed about, searched for." He drew her closer, forgetting all else.

"I love you, Jack." She tossed back her glossy brown hair.

"And I you—dearest."

Time stood still for these two as their emotions rose to fever pitch and took complete charge. Where they were or how they had come there was of no concern. Neither was anything else but this conjoining of two ecstatic mortals, miraculously alive and together—for keeps.

Ultimately returning to the commonplace from their private paradise, they rose up and took stock of their surroundings.

They stood on a slope which Donley recognized as

the one he and the others had soared above when leaving the *Meteoric*, although it now gave mute evidence of the upheaval which had brought Mera and him to the surface of Ormin. There was wreckage here and there; beside them were what was left of the walls of one of the corridors below, distorted and lying in heaps. The floor and ceiling had vanished. Apparently a sideslip of rock strata deep down had been their salvation, unaccountably heaving them to the outside, unharmed. What had led Donley to that precise spot in his last semi-conscious down there, he could not comprehend. But he was more than grateful for the result. He did wonder fleetingly about the side effects of the cosmic pulse which was now no more.

Looking further, what they saw was incredible. There was their own familiar sun overhead, glowing somewhat less bright than on Terra and yet brighter than on Mars. The air was fresh and cool, and downslope from where they stood was the shore of a great body of water, a sea or an ocean. Up the slope was Apdar's plastic dome, a gaping hole in its side and a wide crack extending vertically from the airlock door.

"I don't understand," said Mera. "We were brought up here from the wreck of the *Saturnia*—oh, ages ago. But it wasn't like this. It—"

"Don't try to understand it. I don't either. But I do understand that we're here—"

"—together," Mera supplied, hugging his arm.

"Right." Looking up toward the damaged dome, Donley saw that other survivors were beginning to emerge from the lower regions. "Let's go up and join them, honey."

Together, they picked their way over the ruins, ancient and new. As they drew near, Donley saw Apdar among the group gathered outside the dome, but no one else he recognized. These survivors were some of the formerly living-dead easterners and the others coming up from below were swelling the group rapidly.

Seeing Donley and Mera, Apdar wormed his way through the press and held out his hands. "So glad you saved your lady," he smiled. "And, lady, I tell you this man never gave up. He loves you very much."

Mera's eyes were starry. "I know, Apdar. And I'm glad you're okay, too. You were good to me, I remember." She smoothed back her hair.

Looking around, Donley saw only two or three survivors from the *Meteoric*. "Where's Randall?" he asked Apdar.

Apdar pointed to the top area of the dome. "I supplied him with a protective metal disc on its chain. Like one I wore. This was to postpone living-death till last possible time. He must be up there among the instruments. But the door jammed and I could not break it down."

It was then that Jal Tarjen hove into view and Donley pushed his way through the crowd to collar him. A jammed door, was it?

"Look after Mera!" he called back to Apdar.

CHAPTER TWELVE

But Mera was right there at Donley's heels. And, by the time they had reached the big Martian, others from the *Meteoric* were with him. Lantag was there, Fred and Doris, Phil and Amanda—the survivors from the second ethership were doing all right.

The two honeymoon couples, the Lunarian and the Martian, were all delighted to meet Mera, particularly Jal Tarjen who had seen her under far less happy conditions. They all went into the damaged dome and the two gals, Doris and Amanda, took Mera in hand while the men raced up the spiral stairway. Obviously the three women hit it off at once.

"Get Apdar inside, somebody," Donley called back.

Lantag and Jal Tarjen, rushing it together, broke in the door to the astronomical laboratory which was a shambles. The other three men skittered around the crashed tube and mount of the electron telescope and found Randall pinned under one of the structural members of the assembly. He was unconscious and bleeding but his pulse was strong and his breathing regular.

It took the combined strength of the five men to pry the heavy scope assembly up sufficiently to slide Randall out from underneath. His injuries, it seemed, were similar to those of the man they had brought from the ship, but less extensive. At least Donley hoped that the latter was true.

By now, Apdar had joined them and he soon confirmed Donley's unprofessional diagnosis. "There is a sling," he told them, "and a cable and pulley. Usually used to bring up supplies." As he talked, he moved to a cupboard that had not been damaged, took out the rig he spoke of, then opened a trapdoor in the floor.

"Stand back," he warned. "Very long drop through there."

Using the plastic sling itself as a stretcher, they carried Randall carefully into the operating room as soon as he had been lowered to the floor of the dome. By now the rotunda was crowding with new arrivals from below and the noise of their gay chatter was music to the ears. It had been a long time since such high spirits had pervaded an assembly here. Mera was having the time of her life; some of her friends from the *Saturnia* cruise had evidently joined her little group. Mr. Standish was there and, on seeing the stretcher bearers, he followed into the operating room to assist Apdar as he had done before. Being unable to reach Mera, Donley trailed him in.

He had been deeply concerned about Randall, but now that Apdar had him in hand he felt better. As he had done with the *Meteoric* victim, the amazing leader of the eastern territorials worked swiftly with his very effective instruments. The skull was fractured and this was accompanied by a concussion. But Randall had nothing in addition that was serious, three broken ribs and a couple of smashed toes. In not much more time than it takes to tell, Apdar had completed the brain surgery, healed the ribs and smashed toes, and had Randall awake and ready to get on his feet.

"Hi!" Donley greeted him as he turned his head.

"Donley," he said, "it's good to see you. You too,

Apdar—and Mr. Standish." He sat up and hung his legs over the edge of the operating table. "Let me get outside," he begged. "I want to see just what happened to Ormin."

"Incredible things," smiled Apdar. "It's all right to get on your feet."

"I want you all to know," grunted Randall as he slid to the floor, "that I was not living-dead at any time." He fingered the medallion where it dangled on his bare chest. "I was wide awake when the gaseous body crashed into Ormin. But knocked out when the scope crashed. It was something!"

"It did plenty," Donley assured him. "Wait till you get outside."

The slope was now dotted with survivors, almost down to the water's edge. All milling about and gesticulating. Some mouthing their wonder, many shouting their glee. Breathing deep of the life-giving air. Not questioning the source of their good fortune. That would come later.

"Randall, what do you think?" Apdar asked him.

"It's even better than I'd hoped. And any of my contemporaries back home who try to denounce my theories can go to—the foot of the class."

"Your theories?" Donley was interested to hear more.

"Of the fact of a Plan. Of a universe like a living organism, with a directing intelligence. How else could this have been done? Would any of you say it just happened?"

"No," Donley and the others were forced to agree.

"The damage here is far less than the good accomplished. Because the other body was gaseous the force of the collision was minimized. It struck at precisely the correct angle to start anew the rotation of Ormin. The heat generated was sufficient only to resolve the gases comprising the other body into an atmosphere, what is apparently much water, and undoubtedly other elements necessary to human life. If our calculations were correct, and I assume they were from the appearance of the sun, the new orbit into which Ormin was flung by the collision is between that of Terra and Mars."

"Can't this unbalance the solar system?" asked Donley.

"Not the way the computer analyzed our figures. The new orbit is at just the right angle to the ecliptic and spaced with Ormin in such a position that there'll be no disturbance at all. There may have been a little temporary jolting of the planets, like small quakes, at the time Ormin was driven into its new orbit. That's all, excepting for maybe some unusual tides.

"Now, with the new day and night cycle and a normal yearly orbit around Sol, with the resulting seasons, Ormin should experience such a swift rejuvenation that all life can be on the surface and all the needs of the populace barring the underground minerals and ores be available up here. There'll be vegetation and—"

"Donley put in, "Interplanetary traffic will soon be set up, that's for sure. And if any seeds or animal life other than human are required, these can be brought in."

"You can bet they will be, too," agreed Randall, relaxing now.

Quite a crowd had closed in to hear some of what Randall had been saying and they now began asking questions. This was a signal for Apdar to interfere.

"People," he said in English. "Doctor Randall has just come through a rather serious operation. Is tired. Please no more now."

A sudden thought struck Donley like a blow. Not one of the western territorials had he seen. He felt for Daila's communicator in his pockets. Finding it, he returned to the rotunda and managed to get Mera to one side, away from her bevy of admirers. She saw the communicator in his hand.

"What's that?" she inquired.

"Oh, this," he said. "This goes with a long story and I think you can get the idea better if you listen."

He pressed the buttons of the communicator in their proper sequence and was rewarded by Daila's immediate response. Her voice expressed relief.

"You are all right?" she inquired. "And what of your Mera? My men were waiting when the time of impact came. But you had not arrived with her and I have been unable to make contact mentally with you."

"But how about you and your people? Haven't seen any up here."

"We were cut off from the surface at both ends, by quakes closing the passages. Also, though the shocks at this depth were not as severe, they were of enough violence as to damage their cell doors sufficiently to set free our three prisoners. In fact, they have already slain a guard and made off with the metal box and its mysterious contents. At this moment my workmen are clearing out a new shaft to the lateral tunnel and this will require another two rotations of Ormin to complete."

"Good!" Donley exclaimed. "Then we can count on seeing you soon?"

"Yes. I'm so anxious to meet your Mera. And am delighted with what has happened to the surface of our planet due to its being relocated in the galaxy. Remember my faith, my theories?"

"Indeed I do, Daila."

Looking at Mera, he saw that her heavenly eyes were wide with wonder. He extended the communicator toward her. Here, honey," he said. "Say something to Daila."

"D-Daila?" she said hesitatingly into the device. "I don't even know what half of this is about. Or who you are. Or where. But I'm anxious to meet you."

"Thank you, my dear. Had I but known you were right there, I should have asked to greet you sooner. I shall look forward to our meeting."

"And I too, your maj—. Now why did I say that?"

Daila's tinkling laugh rang out. Jack Donley made the same mistake in the beginning, my dear. But I shall leave it to him to explain to you."

She sounds like a queen, Mera thought, handing the communicator back to Donley. And so she remarked to him before he started speaking.

"Just a second, Daila," he said into the communicator. Then, to Mera, "*Sounds* like a queen, you say? Could you understand her words?"

"Why, why, no, come to think of it, I didn't. How come?" Mera's normally smooth alabaster brow was wrinkled in puzzlement. "But I knew all the time what those foreign words meant."

"Daila," Donley then told the communicator, "my Mera says you *sounded* like a queen."

Again the sparkly laughter. "She is a darling, Jack. I still wish to ask you if you believe that Apdar's people and mine can live in peace?"

"I believe so. But, tell you what I'll do. I'll talk

with Apdar and get his idea. Let you know about it later."

"Excellent. Meanwhile, I would like to make an experiment. My mind tells me you are also a telepathist. By this I mean a *sender*. All humans of intelligence are receptors to some degree. But to be a sender is another thing. Try this for Daila, please; concentrate upon getting a thought to me and do not speak at all. Will you try?"

Donley concentrated. Mightily. But he could think of nothing except Mera. She was here, looking at him with a merry twinkle in her wide eyes. Concentrate as he might, his only thought was of admiration for her and amusement over her openly mischievous look. "She's a rascal, an exquisite little rascal. And she's mine," was all that he could think.

Daila's rippling trill came to them from the communicator which he had set down to be sure it was in no way connected with the test. Now he picked it up again.

"Excellent," came Daila's approval. "I was not wrong, Jack. You sent an extremely clear picture of your Mera and I want more than ever to know her. She is, according to your transmitted thoughts, a lovable girl with a flair for teasing. And you are intrigued by this phase of her nature, proud that she is yours. With training, you can be a master telepathist, but we shall take that up at a later date. Meanwhile, please see what you can do and advise me. Until then, may Providence smile upon you both."

"So that's who you think about me," giggled Mera, who had come very near once more, fingering her silky hair out of the way.

"Yes, you little rascal," he grinned. "Come on now though. Have to see Apdar."

They found Randall and Donley told him the story, that is enough of it to obtain his backing. He also enlisted the help of Jal Tarjen and Standish. Why he should have been so hesitant to approach Apdar in this matter, he was not at all sure.

Especially when he saw the twinkle in Apdar's eyes as he told him about Daila, about the refuge of the western territorials, and of their desire to live in peace —on the surface—with the easterners.

"You believe that I did not know?" Apdar grinned. "Daila thinks I did not know? I laugh. We knew but have been cautious as have they. Now, of course, we will join forces. You tell her?"

"Yes, I'll get the word to her." Donley was delighted.

Donley started for the communicator where it reposed in his pocket. But Mera grasped his wrist to stay the movement of his hand.

"Oh no you don't," she objected. "You have another way, remember?"

Donley gasped. "You mean you went for this telepathisy thing?"

"Yes, even before I heard Daila. I knew, you see, because definite messages came to me from you. Here. When you were still at home on Terra."

"If this is so, try it," Apdar broke in.

Donley tried, perspiration breaking out on his forehead. Then he felt a hand in his pocket. Mera's! She drew out and handed the communicator to him. He pressed the buttons in proper sequence and Daila's voice came in at once.

"Your message came through—strongly. And I am so happy at Apdar's assurance. May I have a word with him?"

Relieved, Donley handed the instrument to Apdar.

Apdar was still conversing animatedly with Daila when the three men, Lantag, Tarjen and Standish, pounced upon Donley and Mera for explanations.

It wasn't easy to convince them.

CHAPTER THIRTEEN

During the succeeding two days, Apdar found many occasions to talk with Daila concerning arrangements to be made for the uniting of East and West. There was first to be a ceremony involving Daila, Apdar, and on each side nine of the most important subjects. Why such conferences were necessary ten or more times a day was not apparent but Donley readily agreed when asked by Apdar for extended use of the communicator.

Grinning, he thought, "If he's so charmed by her voice, wait till he sees her."

At length, Daila and her deputies came through and the ceremony was started by Apdar. Donley watched the leader of the easterners closely as Daila approached him with her train. She was a dream and no mistake, not only ravishingly beautiful but regal in her bearing. Apdar gaped and Donley chuckled as he saw the color rise from his neck to his forehead. Undoubtedly he was smitten—badly.

And this was no side effect of the stellar beat because there was no more of that with which to contend.

The meeting between East and West was held in the repaired rotunda. Clinging to Donley's arm, Mera was wide-eyed watching the proceedings.

"Daila," she gasped, "is the most exquisitely beautiful girl I've ever seen. I had no idea. And young, too. You know, Jack, darn it, I'm jealous."

"Lot of nonsense. You have no reason at all. My contacts with her were—"

"Hah, I know. Strictly business. Well, we'd better get married today, you hear me?" Mera's mischievous twinkle reasserted itself.

Jack Donley knew now that this was precisely what he wanted her to say. "Right," he agreed enthusiastically. "Apdar must have somebody or maybe he can say the words himself."

"Makes no difference who ties the knot. I'm darn tired of us sleeping in separate rooms." Archly, she looked up into his glazing eyes.

"Greedy girl!"

So engrossed had they been in each other and their mutual feeling they had failed to notice that the preliminary meeting of the two leaders and their retinues had ended and festivities were about to begin. Daila and Apdar were coming toward them, smiling.

It was then that Eula and Byrl, with their respective swains, Brand and Davidson, swooped down upon them. Chattering, the girls pounced on Donley, one on either side, holding to his hands and exuding adoration. Abashed, he tried without success to break loose and present Mera. The two young computer programmers were grinning. Like fools. Donley thought.

"See?" said Mera, tongue in cheek. "If I don't tie you down it's going to be just too bad."

The two girls curled their arms around Mera's waist.

Things became a little confused after that. For Daila and Apdar had joined them and others from the *Meteoric* closed in to see what it was all about.

Daila embraced Mera as soon as the young girls released her. "My dear," she said softly. "I heard what you said. And besides, your innermost thoughts were revealed to me."

Mera blushed and Daila trilled her rippling laugh.

"I can tie the knot, my dear," she said, "according to the laws of my people. And this is solemnly binding."

Apdar raised his hand and said a few words in his own tongue. The crowd drew back and formed a circle around their little group, cheering in their own fashion. Daila stood before Jack and Mera, quite obviously to all of them saying the words of a solemn rite as she joined their hands and laid her own hand atop the juncture. They heard them each say, "I do." And then, the two were in a fervent clinch.

A burst of triumphant music came then from the audios. This was like no music of Terra. Neither in its theme nor in the nature of the instruments, but it was stirring and melodious, somehow voicing the joy of two peoples who had joined forces in a new world.

The celebration moved to the outside as more of Daila's subjects arrived from their own environment. It was patent that the westerners were anxious to sniff the outdoor air and to see the sun and the sea they had been told about. They came up ten at a time, since this was the maximum number the tunnel car could accommodate. But already there were twenty in addition to Daila and her attendants and Donley learned that two more of the tunnel cars were being readied.

Down the slope, which had been bulldozed to something like smooth footing, literally hundreds of men, women and children were swarming in the direction of an open stretch of seashore, where a sort of grandstand had been constructed, facing upon a raised platform obviously set up to be used by the leaders of the two territories and their cohorts. A lectern, with microphones, indicated that speeches were expected. A goodly number of poles scattered throughout the area mounted audios that faced in all directions.

Donley caught sight of Doctor Randall making his way toward Daila and Apdar. He appeared to be fully recovered, walking along with accelerated pace. With something on his mind.

Actually, the speeches were not boring. Randall sat on the rostrum, between Apdar and Daila, who talked back and forth across him until he changed seats with Apdar. Mera nudged Donley and was about to make one of her pertinent comments when an easterner who gave the appearance of heading up Apdar's delegation stood up to the microphones.

"You all know why we're here," he said, "and I'll not take any of your time but will immediately present our first speaker, whose beauty and good-will I am sure will impress you. Daila, of our western allies."

"What did he say?" asked Mera. "Wish he'd talk English."

"Probably doesn't know it, even though Apdar does." It was then that Donley realized that his telepathic perception had carried the thought that accompanied the word. This was eavesdropping, he was to learn, since the speaker was not a "sender."

"Just introduced Daila," he whispered to his bride, squeezing her hand. And from that point on, Mera was silent. For she was able to understand every word-thought that issued from the rosebud lips and brilliant mind of Daila. For this one was a telepathisy of superior accomplishment. A sender, receptor, eavesdropper.

Her speech was short and pointedly asking for friendship, assuring her listeners that she and her people had desired for ages past to unite with those of the east—and cooperate. Even to the extent of intermarriage so they would eventually become strictly one people. An acclaim of roaring proportions rose up from the multitude as she ended her plea and sat down.

Apdar's talk was even shorter and in most respects duplicated what Daila had said. He wound up with the positive statement that the union of their peoples was an assured thing and would in fact be as welcome to his people as to hers.

They had noticed that it was getting dark, so intent were all on the proceedings. But now it darkened more swiftly, an eerie fading of the midday light into a deep twilight in which unnatural colors were apparent. A woman looked up and screamed. There was a furor immediately around her and confusions assailed the assemblage as others followed her example and looked toward the sun. It was completely obscured by a shadow of equal size and shape, with long streamers of fire splashing into space on practically all sides of the disc.

These people had never seen nor heard of an eclipse. Evidently Ormin when in orbit around Sirius had no moon.

Randall had been struggling to the microphone and now his calm drawl adjured them. He banged on the lectern with what looked like a gavel and finally got some attention. Apdar was at his side to interpret.

"This is merely an eclipse of the sun," he told them. "A natural phenomenon. Ormin gathered in Ceres, the largest of the planetoids, on its way into the solar system. This is now your moon. Its orbit is quite close

110

and its speed of revolution high. But you will have such eclipses of the sun and others of the moon itself occasionally. I had determined these facts with Apdar's instruments, the undamaged ones, and that is why I forced my way to this stage. Take it easy now; there is absolutely no danger. See, the sun is even now being uncovered."

It was true, a brilliant crescent was renewing the lost daylight, gradually but surely, and it widened rapidly until the entire orb of the sun was revealed.

"Don't we learn something every day though," Mera said, more as a statement than a question. "Who'd have thought Ormin would capture a moon and give us a show so soon after getting put?"

Donley laughed a little shakily. He had been afraid of a stampede of these people of Ormin who had not known what to expect. And it was a reaction for which he could hardly blame them, even had he been so inclined. This generation was faced with enough adjusting to do, merely getting used to the day and night demarcation by the rising and setting of the sun, adapting themselves to the cool invigorating breezes.

Daila was beckoning them to the platform, where the dignitaries were now gathering in relaxed groups.

Reminding him that the escaped prisoners were still at large, Daila suggested that he and Mera return with her to her buried city. "They're unable to leave," she advised, "because the new exit is heavily guarded against just that. But they haven't been found yet and so are potentially very dangerous, besides which I think your people should have them. The first of their murders, to our knowledge, was aboard your ship."

"Right. Okay if Jal Tarjen comes along?"

"Of course."

111

Jack hesitated. Then he added, "How about Lantag?"

"Excellent. And Mera and I can get really acquainted while you men go chasing criminals."

So Donley rounded up the Lunarian and the Martian, noting during his search that construction of the new city along the shore was again in full blast and had proceeded famously already. Apdar's workmen were real craftsmen and fast. Later, of course, many of Daila's workers would be here to join them.

The trip down and through the tunnel was uneventful. Donley saw that the rest of the seats in the car were occupied by some of Apdar's people.

"The first for exchange," Daila explained when he remarked upon this. "You see, Apdar and I agreed on an exchange of easterners and westerners in equal numbers, then rotating at the halfway mark. This will be of educational value to all and give each side a clearer understanding of the other, besides giving all the chance to spend some time on the surface. You undoubtedly saw on your way down back there that the living quarters had scarcely been damaged, although in some of the lower levels there was some destruction, mainly in the tilting and buckling of walls and floors here and there. Very forunate. Also that the utilities are functioning perfectly, apparently unharmed. But the thing is that there are accommodations back there for only fifty-two hundred people, as far as sleeping, eating, ablutions and recreational facilities are concerned. And there are four thousand of my people, plus about five thousand of Apdar's, so they can not possibly reside in either place all at one time. It was for this reason we made the exchange agreement. And when the new tunnel cars are ready we can speed this up, since not only are they faster but each will hold

112

fifty passengers. Of course, as soon as the new city is habitable all of us will live there—until population increase or the spirit of adventure, or newcomers from the other planets inspire exploration and the establishing of other dwelling places."

"You two sure did some planning," said Donley. "No wonder you were talking back and forth so much those two days."

Daila blushed charmingly, at sight of which Mera hugged her and said, "So-o. Maybe you and Apdar— just might—"

The girls indulged in some animated whispering then and Donley tossed a pleased grin back at Lantag and the Martian. Who knew what might happen? An aftermath of the cosmic pulse, was it all?

Finally the car came to rest a new gravity lift shaft and they were dropped speedily down this to the inner world occupied for so many generations by the western territorials. Excepting for the guards, the corridors were deserted. It was sleeping time here. A guard approached after the girls had entered Daila's chambers and told Donley that the escaped prisoners were last seen along one of the balconies several levels below.

"Let's go," Donley said.

CHAPTER FOURTEEN

Reaching the level indicated, they heard a shot and Captain Stark reeled from a branching corridor almost into Donley's arms. Two more of Daila's guards had joined the first one on the way down, and the three spread out with Lantag and Jal Tarjen to search the passages. Stark warned that the thugs were close by and then he collapsed. A door nearby opened and two citizens, a man and wife, peered out to see what the commotion might be. Donley asked them to put the captain in one of their beds until he could get medical help. They readily agreed, having heard all of the proceedings at the new seaside, and Donley was free again to join the chase. Regaining consciousness briefly before Donley left, Stark gave him the apartment number of their hideout.

"It's right around the corner," he husked, "and you should find them not too far away." Then he slipped again into dreamland.

The Martian was just rounding the corner into the corridor, moving cautiously, his eyes darting here and there in search of the hoodlums.

"No sight of them yet?" Donley asked.

"Not yet. Lantag and guards scour all passages."

Just then it happened. The two escapees hove into view and, seeing Donley and the Martian, one fired a shot that went wild and both turned to flee. Donley and Jal Tarjen sped after them.

Donley launched himself in a flying tackle that brought one of the fugitives crashing to the metal floor. Meanwhile, the Martian had caught the other and was using a trick reminiscent of karate, tossing the man over his shouler to smash into unconsciousness.

At this point the three guards converged upon them and shackled their captives.

"Where's the wounded one?" asked the first guard.

Donley made reply, coupled with swift instructions.

"I'll get help for him and bring him to the tunnel car. Meanwhile, you two get the steel box from their hideout and bring it along with them to join us." He selected two of the guards as he spoke. "And you," he told the other, "stay with us while we take care of the wounded one; then you'll be free to return to your post."

They found that the helpful citizens had already had in a doctor and that Stark's wound had been cleansed, the bullet extracted, and all bandaged up in approved manner.

"You may take him with you," the doctor told them. "He's had a hypo that will keep him under for a few hours and then you'll need another doctor to look at him. He'll recover with proper care."

Instinctively, Donley knew it would be an insult to offer compensation, so he simply thanked the couple and the doctor. Captain Stark was picked up easily by Lantag and Jal Tarjen, who carried him away with extreme care toward the new exit.

"I'll join you at the car," Donley told them, "in nothing flat. Have to tell Daila what went on and bring her and Mera along."

He sped to the upper level where Daila's quarters were located.

The two women were in a state of mild excitement when he reached them. Daila had eavesdropped telephatically. She knew what had ben done, all of it, so congratulated him on their coup.

"But guess what," gurgled Mera, "one of the big cars is ready and we'll be taking a whole lot of Daila's people back with us. We get a faster ride, too."

The new car was indeed fast, beyond the speed of sound. In the confines of the tunnel, sonic boom seemed not to be feared, possibly because there was not enough surrounding air to generate one. At least any audible result of shock waves would be left far behind them. Donley would have to ask Randall to be sure of this, although they had certainly heard nothing of the sort and were less than a half hour reaching the western terminal. Using these new cars would greatly speed up the exchange of Daila's and Apdar's people.

The two prisoners, surly and mouthing curses, were left manacled and were temporarily locked into separate rooms off the rotunda which were ordinarily used for equipment storage but were now empty on account of the construction work outside.

Captain Stark was taken to Apdar's operating room and laid on the table, where the eastern leader proceeded to examine his wound and check his pulse and respiration. Temperature as well. Stark was still under the influence of the hypodermic injection but was declared by Apdar to be in good shape.

"Your doctor," he told Daila, "did fine with him. The man will get well. Can move him to room down below. I see him again when he wakes."

Randall had come in to join them as Lantag and the Martian carried Stark out. "We put him in my bed," Lantag was saying, "until his own ready."

"What's the story about Stark and the two others?" Randall wanted to know.

They repaired to an adjoining room, a sort of library where plenty of comfortable seats were available. Mr. Standish and the steward had joined them, having learned of their arrival with the captain.

"The story," Donley began, "is a long one but I think when it's all considered we can rule Stark out as a confederate. Tarjen here recognized the two crooks from the *phobos* and it was they who forced Stark to knock out the steward, forced him to take them in the escape ship, and now have shot him. They're safely locked up and the question is what to do with them."

Daila made a suggestion: "Would it not be a good idea to open the metal box and see what it is they have stolen?"

Everybody agreed and her two guards set the box before them on a table. Apdar, after going out for some tools, managed to pry open the lid. There in neat packages, labeled with the Venusian word *Evoro* was a fortune in the narcotic drug which was having such devastating effect on the youth of both Terra and Mars.

"Several million credits' worth!" gasped Donley. "No wonder they wanted to get away with it!"

Daila's thought-words disclaimed any hold on the prisoners after this revelation. "I'm certain they will pay for all of their crimes, including those against my subjects. Return them with the first ship that comes here from your world."

They agreed solemnly and Apdar offered the use of a pair of cells for their safe-keeping until the day of departure for Terra. Cells, he said which had not been used for generations.

As they broke up the meeting and started across the rotunda, the floor quivered heavily beneath their feet, the entire dome overhead swayed violently and there were the crashes of heavy objects toppling to the floor back in the library and in other side rooms.

"An earthquake!"

The Orminese, both eastern and western territorials, seemed to be about ready to panic. Outside on the slope arose a babbling of shouts and cries, some of them hysterical. And the sounds of construction down at the shore ceased, pile drivers and bulldozers being deserted by their operators. Daila and Apdar kept cool, as befitted their station, and followed Randall and Donley as they rushed out over the weaving floor to see what could be done to quiet the fears of the populace. Apdar steered Randall to a microphone stand just outside, explaining that it operated the audios that had been erected for the ceremonies as well as the system in the levels below.

In a very few seconds the temblor subsided and the ground beneath them was steady once more. But the slope was a shambles of terrified humanity, scurrying hither and yon, not knowing which way to turn for safety from this phenomenon they could only interpret as a further calamity of planet-wide proportions.

Randall was shouting into the mike, with Apdar interpreting after him, "Hold it everybody! This is only a quake caused by shifting of rock or soil strata that were disturbed during the great collision. There may be more shocks, but there's little to fear if you just stay away from heavy structures or objects that could topple upon you. Stay away from underneath anything which might be dislodged and crush you."

But this generation of Orminese had never experienced anything like this before. Consequently it was not easy to convince them. Especially since a secondary temblor followed almost immediately.

However, after a little more exhortation over the audio systems all was quiet once more. But Donley had a feeling of impending trouble, of what sort he could not imagine.

Randall and Mr. Standish had been closeted together with Apdar in the laboratory section of the upper dome for about half a day when Donley became curious and climbed the circular stair himself. Just in time to hear a shout from the mate.

"That's it! That's it! The *Meteoric!*" he exulted. "Of all the good luck, on an island."

"Luck, Mr. Standish? That a limitless sea should come to surround the ship and an island be supplied to hold it above water. This you call luck? I say it is part of a Plan. Remember?" Randall was back on his favorite theme.

Somehow, now it made sense to Donley. He thought fleetingly of the cosmic pulse as he saw that they had located the vessel with electronic feelers and optical scanners. But how would they get to it?

He must have been exercising his telepathic "sending" ability without intention, for as if in answer to his question Apdar said, "We can get to it by using the rocket packs. From space suits."

"Right. We sure can," said Randall, "and let's do it—now. Let's look over the damage and see if it can be repaired."

"Okay if I come along?" Donley asked from the doorway.

Surprised, the three looked around at him. All three grinned and voiced assent, each in his own way.

He kept close to Randall as they went below and

selected rocket packs that held sufficient fuel from the heap in the storeroom. A small crowd gathered to see them off as, one by one, they rose on the twin exhausts of the rocket tubes. It was but a few minutes to the *Meteoric*.

A quick inspection showed a considerable stretch of hull plates on the bottom torn loose, a few of these buckled beyond repair but the rest merely needed to be welded in place. The hull bracing was intact.

Returning to the dome, Apdar turned his attention to the radio equipment he had been experimenting with before the coming of the ray stream and the steller beat.

"This," he told them, "was intended to be used for interplanetary communication. But put out of commission by cosmic energy. We try it now."

"Try point two five megacycles frequency," Randall suggested, "with call letters WSA-1000. That's World Space Authority headquarters."

Apdar translated this into his own standards and made some dial settings, then closed a switch that set a motor-generator singing and lighted the panel of the radio. He pulled down a headset very much like those used on earth, clamped it over his ears and started a monotonous refrain.

"Calling WSA-1000, calling WSA-1000, Planet Ormin calling WSA-1000, calling WSA-1000."

Apdar threw the send-receive switch and they all listened with bated breath. Nothing came through the audio excepting the crackling of static.

He tried again. "Planet Ormin calling WSA-1000, calling WSA-1000—"

Again the switch was thrown and again all of them

listened, but not for long. Faintly there came the words, "Come in Planet Ormin. Over."

It *was* World Space Authority Headquarters. Apdar replied, asking for a tuning signal. It came back, "WSA-1000 testing, WSA-1000 testing," repeated at least ten times. Apdar tuned carefully and brought in the voice strongly by the time the speaker had come to the final "over."

"Thank you WSA-1000," said Apdar. "I read you fine. Telling you Doctor Randall is here and wants to report. Over."

"Roger, Planet Ormin," came the response. "We'll get Colonel Reyn on here. Meanwhile will have call letters and number assigned for your use. Here is the colonel—"

Another voice came on, deeper, more authoritative. "You there, Randall?" it asked. "Been wondering about you. Come in with your report please. Over."

A long conversation followed, developing the facts that the WSA had determined the orbit, position and many physical data regarding their planet. They had been tracing it since the *Meteoric* first reported and now had two etherships on the way to rescue the survivors. Randall reported the capture of the two narcotic runners and was informed of their importance as two of the principals in the combine which had been only partially broken up. The recovery of the contraband is likewise good news to WSA and other authorities.

Randall told of the two civilizations of Ormin, a little of their past history and of their joining forces on the surface since the collision which had rejuvenated their planet.

While the conversation was going on, Donley held

up a card on which he had pencilled, "Ask when the rescue ships arrive."

Randall's question in this regard elicited the information that eighteen days of Ormin's time would still be required for the journey. "Be sure you have landing facilities readied by then," the colonel added.

"We'll be ready, Sir," was Randall's final word. "Signing off."

Jack returned quickly to Mera with news of the rescue ships. But he did not tell her of the renewed enmities on earth. This could wait; it was enough that he worry about it in secret.

Even the slightest possibility of a nuclear disaster to Terra such as the past had brought to Ormin was unthinkable. It could not be.

CHAPTER FIFTEEN

In ten days time, much was accomplished.

Dailapdar, the new city by the sea, was already taking shape. Public squares, broad avenues with four-lane moving ways in each direction, walkways along the sea front, had been laid out in accordance with a detailed plan worked out by the hastily formed city planning board. This board had members from both east and west and had retained as advisor a celebrated architect from Terra who had been a passenger on the *Saturnia*. Main and side streets of residential areas of the city, as well as many dissimilar models of houses and apartments were being designed by this architect.

Construction shanties outlined the area and grading, excavation, the setting of foundations, even the erection of structural steel columns for the public buildings, was well under way. Heavy construction equipment brought up through new large size lift shafts from both the eastern and western communities were in constant use, day and night, in addition to which new equipment manufacture had been started in mills and foundries built along the shore outside the city limits. A scene of tremendous activity was to be observed by day or night and the close cooperation of artisans and workmen of various trades helped greatly in speeding the fraternization of the easterns and westerns.

There seemed to be an almost irresistible attraction between young men of the east and young women of the west—and vice versa. Already, a number of inter-marriages were planned, making it obvious even at this early stage that complete integration of the two races would not be long in coming. Actually, there were scarcely any noticeable differences in physical appearance between the two, or in their way of think-ing. Even their spoken tongues were enough alike as to make communication a simple matter, assisted a little over any difficult spots by the thought-transference training of the westerners. This younger generation was already considering itself as comprised of neither easterners nor westerners but Orminese. And using the term in public. It was truly a one world concept. And a population explosion was sure to ensue.

It was at about this time that Daila and Apdar an-nounced over the audio systems that they planned an immediate personal union. The reason was apparent at once, the statement being received with good-humored disbelief by both the Orminese and their visitors from the other planets. For had not many of them seen the glances that passed between the two in public? Actu-ally the mating of the two rulers was hailed as a royal romance that would weld solidly the new alliance and make their people as one.

Construction of a spaceport several miles from the city limits had been started with the news of the com-ing of the WSA etherships and was proceeding, if anything, at an even greater rate than that of the city. It was to provide two landing cradles in the beginning, then later to be expanded to a total of ten. Dailapdar was anticipating a very considerable interplanetary traffic, and rightly so.

But, with all of this activity and with the evidence of a bright future for Ormin and the Orminese, there developed a strange unrest among several of the *Meteoric's* survivors. Mera had noticed this and, puzzled by it, called it to Donley's attention. It appeared to be an unreasonable and quite unwarranted feeling. It was not exactly a demonstration of fear but rather like an attack of extreme nostalgia. Even of morbid depression in one instance, the case of the *Meteoric's* steward, who kept to himself almost constantly and hardly responded when greeted by those with whom he had become friendly on board ship and later here. The married couples, Fred and Doris, Phil and Amanda, did not appear to be affected but did seem to prefer their own company to any other. "Can't say I blame them," Donley said with a grin, swiftly taking Mera in his arms.

For a long sweet moment they forgot the new problem. But then it was brought to their attention in no uncertain manner. The chime called them to the door of their apartment and there stood Lantag.

"You're stoned," Mera accused him, for he was swaying on his feet.

"Not so," the Lunarian denied. And Mera knew instantly that this was the truth because the man slumped against her and his breath was as sweet as a baby's. "Not so," Lantag repeated. "It is cosmic pulse, come back."

"Wh-at?" Mera cocked her head but could discern nothing at all to resemble the *lub-dub*, *lub-dub* refrain. Neither could Donley.

Mera was aflutter with the desire to be helpful. She remembered the stellar beat from what now seemed long ago. Remembered it as something that pounded at her nerves until she thought she'd go insane. And then, mercifully, she had known no more. Excepting for dreams she could not now recall.

Slumped in a chair, Lantag seemed to be sleeping peacefully. Not in any sense like the living-death. His color hadn't changed and his breathing seemed to be quite normal.

"Let's get to Randall about this," Mera suggested. Donley agreed, and carried Lantag to the sofa, where they left him in slumber.

They found Randall with Apdar—and Daila—in the electronics lab. In the top portion of the dome. Mera was telling them about Lantag. Donley let her do the talking, she was so eager.

"Strange," drowled Randall. "It's this sort of thing we've been investigating. Noticed some of these odd goings on."

"Any idea what it is?" asked Donley, not seeming too concerned.

"Not yet. Remember we never did know the precise nature of the throb. Apdar here even claimed to be its originator."

Apdar grinned sheepishly. "Forget my little conceit, please," he begged them. "Suppose I thought I could control my people better that way. But now—" He spread his hands in a helpless gesture.

"You think Lantag's case might help?" asked Donley.

"Well he sounds like the worst of them," opined Randall. "And yet, so far, we've been unable to identify the thing was of electrical origin. How do we test Lantag, or anybody else?"

Daila's amazing violet eyes were wide with question. "Might it be that telepathic eavesdropping would—?"

"That's it!" exclaimed Apdar. "Sure as can be. No

matter what the source, it is a brian image. So we try, right?"

He looked to Randall for agreement. "I'll try anything once. Do we bring him here?"

"If you say it isn't electrical in nature. Why not all go down to our apartment. Where Lantag is."

But Lantag was not where they had left him. Evidently awkening and finding himself alone, he had left for parts unknown.

He was not in his qwn rooms either, as they soon learned. His door was left wide open and this was cause for mild alarm. In his condition anything could happen to him.

"The steward's rooms are right across from here," Donley offered. "Let's see if he's in."

The steward answered their ring, long-faced. Dour. Not at all his usual self. "What do all of you want with me?" he asked.

"Like to talk with you," Randall made answer. "May we come in?"

"Suit yourself." Leaving the door open, the steward weaved to a chair and sat there, a melancholy and uncommunicative figure. He did not even look up as the three men and two women found seats for themselves.

"Are you looking forward to going home?" Donley asked him, to break the uncomfortable silence. He saw that Daila was concentrating mightily.

The steward shrugged. "Guess so."

Just then the door chime sounded and their unwilling host made no move to answer its summons. Apdar let in Mr. Standish.

The mate looked at the steward where he sat, then at the others. "Mind if I take a look at him?"

"Of course not," said Randall. Apparently the mate

had not been affected by whatever it was and had been keeping tabs on the steward.

They watched as he inserted a fever thermometer in his mouth and took his pulse, then rolled back the lids and peered into his eyes with a penlite flash. After another minute, he took out the thermometer and squinted at its scale.

"Normal! Everything normal. Yet something's wrong with the man. I don't get it."

"Possibly psychosomatic?" Donley asked.

"Just possibly," Standish admitted. "But there's something—"

They saw that Daila had relaxed, eyes shining. She was shaking her head, rising to say something, when the steward sort of shuddered and collapsed in his chair.

Before any of them could get to him, the audios blared forth in the strident alarm which called for all on the surface to take cover at once. Apdar paled perceptibly; he had expected that this alarm would never be needed.

A host of frightened humanity was crowding through the great double doors from outside into the rotunda. And a brilliant pyrotechnic display in the night sky was quickly seen as the cause of the debacle. Apdar and his companions hastened to the astronomical laboratory up top. Better than through the transparent dome wall, they could see in the disc of the optical scanner what proved to be a meteor shower of giant proportions and brightness.

The audio systems were alive with the voice of Apdar, explaining the phenomeon and telling all within hearing that there was small chance of any danger, that these meteor showers were occasionally experienced on all the planets having an atmosphere. The flaming trains, he explained, were caused by the complete burning up of the bodies by atmospheric friction and so they never reached the ground. Excepting in very rare cases. The visitors from other planets were familiar in such phenomena, he told his own people and Daila's.

Just at this point, a particularly large, comet-like visitant arched all the way through the atmosphere and landed far out in the sea with a thunderous impact and the spouting of a brilliantly illuminated geyser of water. The first meteorite! And no harm done. The show was over in another moment, the last of the dwindling shower fading into nothingness.

A combined sigh of relief rose from the huge crowd in the rotunda and they began pouring through the exits somewhat shamefacedly, returning to their labors.

Daila had been talking in animated whispers with Mera and now that the fireworks were over she spoke up.

"The steward," she told them, "was in a state of similar to shock, with his conscious thought mostly submerged in and controlled by the subconscious. A thought-image I clearly picked up did carry a pulsation similar to the one you have described as a cosmic or stellar throb or beat. I checked this against my own pulse and found they coinsided closely. But flashing across this image at frequent intervals was a fleeting impression of anticipated release, this being accompanied by a sence of withdrawal from a sparkling shower not too unlike the meteoric display we just witnessed. The original thought-image I extracted may have been a memory-image, a recollection of the actual cosmic pulse previously felt. On the other had—there seemed to be—I could sense another entity."

"You think it could be related to the natural phenomenon we just witnessed?" Donley put in. "I did vaguely pick up something of the sort, not with image clarity such as yours, of course."

Daila patted his hand. "You are coming along fine," her thought-words approved.

"Let's get this straight," said Randall, seeing that Apdar was in sort of a daze of wonderment, just staring admiringly at Daila. "You infer you were able to read all of this in the steward's mind? As we sat there?"

"Exactly. And I hope you can interpret it because I can't."

Randall frowned. "Give me time," he begged. "This is something way out, as far as I'm concerned. Doesn't fit in with science.My kind of science."

It was then that Lantag came clumping up the spiral stair, walked briskly across the platform and entered the room. He was normal, himself once more.

"Why everybody so solemn?" he inquired.

That broke up the session. "I'll do some more thinking," Randall promised Daila.

"And I too," said Apdar. "But it's time for sleep now, and we all need it, I'm sure."

But no interpretation of Daila's eavesdropping was forthcoming the following day, nor the day after that. And all of those who had been affected by the mysterious epidemic had recovered entirely. In fact, they did not seem to know they had been through anything of account at all, not one of them mentioing it.

Then came the day the WSA ships were due to arrive from Luna. The two cradles at the spaceport were ready to accommodate them and the control tower was in service, its transmitters tuned to the frequency of WSA receivers. Back at the end of the field, where the last of the ten cradles would be located, was the radar antenna, rotating endlessly. It was amazing to all how speedily and thoroughly the job had been completed. These Orminese were dedicated and conscientious artisans.

Captain Stark had completely recovered and was around and about. He was extremely interested in all he saw but had very little to say, it being quite obvious that he was a bit apprehensive as to what might be the decision in his regard when WSA ships came in. He had been given a clean bill by Randall and the mate, but he knew the final decision was up to WSA authorities.

Quite a large group was assembled in the administration building main waiting room well in advance of the time when the first of the two etherships was to land. Most of survivors of the *Meteoric* and the *Saturnia* were on hand, in addition to Daila and Apdar with their retinues and some of the older and younger Orminese who were not in the working force. Those working on the new city and in the fields had refused a holiday, saying they could see the vessels approach from where they worked.

Preliminary warning of the approach of the first ship came in the form of the roar of braking rockets increasing gradually from inaudibility to deafening intensity. The ship came into view in the east, its sleek shape driving down at a steep angle and visibly decelerating. It must have circled Ormin at least twice in a tight spiral to come down from the upper reaches at this angle and its speed had now reduced to practically a standstill. It was probably two thousand feet up, Donley guessed, when it circled the cradle which had been marked for its landing, then swung back slowly to hover directly above it with rockets blasting in all directions but up. So slowly and carefully did its pilot drop it on multiple jets that it settled into the cradle without an audible bump. Out of sight now behind the barrier that held in the discharge of its flaming jets.

Abruptly the jets shut off and you could hear the silence. The barrier started dropping and the huge blowers outside began clearing the landing area of burned rocket gases.

Only when the signal clanged did the building doors open to allow the crowd to rush out toward the landing cradle.

The first rescue ship was on Ormin!

CHAPTER SIXTEEN

By the time the second WSA ship was cradled, Captain Stark had been cleared by top officialdom of the all-powerful agency, without whose approval he would have been finished as master of an ethership. All had been arranged by ship radio after the captain of the WSA-18, the first ship to arrive, had heard the stories of Daila, Randall and Donley, as well as of two of Daila's guards. This was done quite informally and of course the captain was a new man when told of the decision. Stark's old testiness was a thing of the past.

The metal box with its contents of Evoro, the Venusian narcotic of such fearsome capability, was safely in the vault of the ship's purser. The two killers who had tried to get away with it were in the brig, manacled and with leg-irons. They were taking no more chances with this slippery and dangerous pair. WSA headquarters in Los Angeles heated the ether with congratulatory messages.

News cameras and reporters from World Television and the TV chains of Venus and Mars had come along and were already interviewing Daila, Apdar and Doctor Randall. All of whom had given credit for the capture of the gunmen to Jack Donley. So a news reporter and cameraman went looking for Donley and Mera, another crew for Captain Stark. Before they were finished they would have them all on tape—or else. Having learned that the singer, Doris Bright was on the *Meteoric's* passenger list, a special team was running her down. They'd have her charming person and one or more of her songs on tape—for free, outside of her contract with World TV. For now she was news, too.

Visitors to both ships went aboard in lines, many of them Orminese who were curious to see the internals. The survivors had been extended the privilege of communication with their people by radio, to whichever planet it was necessary to make the call. Without obligation, of course. All seemed to be taking advantage of the offer, thereby relieving the worries of loved ones at home, besides enabling the passengers to discuss their immediate plans.

Eula and Byrl, among the first to use the radiophone, carried on long and gurgling conversations with their parents, who were delighted to know they were safe as well as being more than pleased with the turn of events. Especially with the girl's obvious enthusiasm regarding the two young men, Brand and Davidson. And when told that the latter were extending their vacations and likewise going to the planet Mars, they readily gave their blessing and permission for the girls to continue to Risapar, their originally intended destination. Additional funds would be waiting for them there, they were assured.

Lantag's call was a simple one but decisive. He talked with his superior in the Lunar spaceport, and resigned from his position there as a maintenance mechanic. He had decided to remain in Ormin, being already employed in the construction work in Dailapdar.

Through the captain of the WSA-6, the second ship to arrive, Jal Tarjen had received the offer of first mate's berth on a new ship of the Mars-Venus run and he used his call to accept. Delighted with the chance.

Doctor Randall discussed his immediate future with his superiors back in LA and was granted his expressed wish to remain for a time on Ormin to have a long session with Apdar in connection with the design and use of certain of his astronomical and surgical instruments that are different and in many ways superior to those in use on Terra or the other planets.

Mera had fully expected that she and Jack would return. But Donley, for some reason of his own, was delaying the decision. Which was okay with Mera. She loved the guy and whatever was all right with him would be all right with her. Where he goes, that is my place, was her decision.

Arrangements were being made for the repairs to the *Meteoric* and Captain Stark's discussions with her owners had resulted in agreements to keep Mr. Standish, the steward, the other crew members and himself on the payroll. Present cargo, if unharmed, was to be continued to its original destination and additional cargo from Ormin could be taken on if available. It was a most satisfactory arrangement to all of them and those who had families back home were able to notify them of their well being and future plans.

Phil Carter, having been employed in the warehouse department of the Dailapdar construction force, resigned his old cargo tracer job and he and Amanda decided to become adopted Orminese, at least for a while. Amanda's feelings in this respect were very much like Mera's, She could be happy anywhere with Phil.

WSA officers from the two ships were conferring daily with Apdar and Daila, then with their top advisors, listing commodities needed by the Orminese and which were available on the other planets. It seemed that a brisk interplanetary trade would result in not too long a time.

Ormin was to prove a valuable addition to the solar system.

In far-off Vloreg, Shalag, Keeper of the Records for so long, was preparing his successor to take over. Krylin, ages younger than his mentor, was rated second only to Vloreg in technical ability and so was considered a worthy inheritor of the important post and the logical choice.

Shalag was projecting for the education of his temporary protege his tape of the recent collision of two bodies out there in space, the collision which had resulted in the hurling of a long-dead world into a new orbit in Vastar 181-x and renewing it life.

"You will observe," he told his pupil, "that at the moment of impact and resultant breaking down of the gases comprising the second of the bodies, a new rotation was imparted to the dead world so that is was able to take its place as a habitable body in its adopted solar system. A new atmosphere as well. I maintain that all this was conceived and implemented by the central intelligence that controls our universe.

"You have seen the energy streams that carried the two bodies to their meeting. Since this tape was made, I have determined by spectroscopic and oscillographic as well as other means, that the blue beam propelling the dead world, carried superimposed upon it a most amazing energy, a throbbing pulse which comprised several healing properties as well as an anaesthetic one which provided a deep sleep for all humans of the east when the collision occurred. Its healing constituents were psychological, medical, even hypnotic in nature.

Many personalities of humans were completely altered, gloomy natures became joyful, slaves to a vice became free of it, some without love in their hearts acquired it.

"I have likewise determined that the dead world was dead only on its surface, two civilizations having lived underground and multiplied for many generations after the surface had been blasted by the foolish and futile nuclear warrings of their ancestors. What the healing properties of the superimposed energies have accomplished, I shall now demonstrate to you in the viewplate of the galactic scanner."

Using powerful magnification, Shalag brought to the lighted viewplate first a portion of the blasted surface of Ormin, then moving along until the vast expanse of the new sea could be seen as far as the horizon. Following the seashore and increasing magnification, he stopped next at the spaceport where numbers of people could be seen moving back and forth between a large building and two space ships in their landing berths.

Further shifting of the view and increased magnification showed an extremely busy scene at the construction site of what was to be a large city at the water's edge. The orderly movement of materials and of men who performed the various required labors, as well as the speed with which the work proceeded drew expressions of approval from Krylin.

"These people are descendants of once warring ancestors?" he asked wonderingly.

"They are."

"One would not suspect it from the unity with which they labor side by side."

"You are quite right, my son. Now observe and perhaps you will note some of the reasons."

The scanner's field of view shifted up the slope to a transparent dome, then with further increase of

137

magnification went inside. Shalag manipulated a control lever as they focussed on a group of people, two men and two women, all of them handsome and bright of visage. The control Shalag was using brought in their speech, as well as its telepathic interpretation.

"Two of there are rulers of the now united people," Shalag stated. "The beautiful blonde woman and the red-haired man. Each was leader of a faction of those whose ancestors were such rivals in science and such bitter enemies that they destroyed themselves and their outer world."

"Who are the other two?" Krylin asked.

"These are from the next inner world of Vastar 181-x and have become lifemates here. What I mainly wanted you to note, however, is that two of these are quite versatile telepathists, more particularly the woman, the empress we might call her. Daila by name."

Shalag lighted another screen and the mental processes of the one called Daila showed up in swirls of varying colors that meant much to these scientists of Vloreg. The extra-sensory capabilities of the woman were clearly outlined in a manner understandable to them.

"She is quite amazingly endowed," agreed Krylin. "It is apparent that she is able to project, to absorb and to pilfer thoughts of another from a distance. Show me the other."

The view changed and the swirls shown were of different form and color. "This is the man from the other world who is called Jack Donley," his tutor told Krylin.

After a moment, Krylin said in astonishment, "This one has most exceptional power of projecting, not only his own thoughts but facets of his own nature, and without the subject being able to resist or later remember. The other capabilities need further development."

Shalag smiled approvingly. "You have insight, my son," he said, "and I fear not for your future in my stead. No doubt you will watch the progress of these people on their rejuvenated world when I have gone."

"Thank you, indeed," his pupil replied humbly. "I shall watch them."

"Now to the next inner world of Vastar 181-x," said Shalag.

Daila was explaining the thought transference process which enabled her people to convey their meaning as they spoke to those who did not understand their language.

"The words are usually necessary," she said, "since they are the carriers of the thoughts, not a telepathic projection from the speaker's mind. Only a very few of my subjects beside myself have the ability to project at all, and these not over great distances. Apdar, forgive me for using the term 'my subjects.' It's in the past tense, of course; they're our subjects now."

"I understand, my dear," gravely from Apdar.

Donley and Mera were listening intently.

"Tell me, Daila," Donley queried, "it's a matter of training, isn't it? I mean, it would be if I, for instance, wanted to increase my telepathic abilities, wouldn't it?"

"Yes, training will help."

"But where to get it."

"Right here. A man named Rojan, although not a marvelous telepathist himself, is an extremely good instructor. You know many of the best vocal teachers are not exceptional singers, and this seems to be a parallel. But it would take a period of several months, although you have a fine start already."

139

Mera was looking sidewise at her man. What did he have in mind?

"I would like to try something," Donley offered. "I want to talk to Randall about this and I'd like to try and bring him here—telepathically."

"I'd love to see you do it," Daila told him.

Mera held her breath as he concentrated consulted her wristwatch. One minute. Two minutes. Three. F— no, not quite four minutes. And Randall walked into this private gallery that looked out through the transparent wall of the dome top toward Dailapdar and the sea.

"I got the impression that you want to see me, Donley," Randall said in a voice that was small for him. He was scratching his head perplexedly.

"Randall, I *put* the impression there," Donley faltered, "and I've got to confess to something."

"Confess?" Mera thought her ears deceived her.

"Yes, and to you all. But to Randall especially. Randall, have you found any explanation for the little epidemic we seemed to have a while back, like with Lantag and the steward—their condition then?"

"No, I haven't. In fact, haven't thought about it too much."

"Glad you haven't. Because I did that." Donley caressed his chin.

"You did *what?*" They all turned to Donley, not quite understanding.

"I projected those replicas of the cosmic pulse into their think tanks and this is why I apologize. I didn't mean to deceive you all, I just wanted to find out how far I could go with this—this—"

"As far as I'm concerned, you don't need to apologize," Daila said sweetly. "No harm was done. And you did succeed."

140

"Yes, with several more. But those were the outstanding ones. It was a fluke, the fireworks I put in their thoughts almost coinciding with the meteor shower. I was thinking not of meteors but of star-burst rockets such as we use in celebrations. At any rate, I brought them all back to normal—but quick! And they don't seem to remember."

The appreciative laughter that followed relieved Donley's mind greatly since it showed him there was no resentment.

"Honey," Mera said softly, "please go on. Tell us *why* you want to improve your ESP."

"Sorry dear—I had to plan it this way. And here's why. Maybe I'm bats, maybe you'll think I picture myself as a bigshot, which I'm sure as hell not. But what the captain of the WSA-18 has been telling me about conditions politically on Terra has fired me up. He says we're on the brink again of nuclear war and I have a hunch I may be able to do something to help avert it. With projected thought in the right places. Think I'm dreaming?"

"No!" came a chorus of approval, including Mera's.

"Then, Daila," he said, "I'm staying here for instruction."